J·M· CELI

THE VAMPIRES OF 1863

Published by Rockamooka Press
Bellingham, Massachusetts

ISBN# 979-8-9884930-5-1 | eBook
ISBN# 979-8-9884930-3-7 | Paperback
ISBN# 979-8-9884930-4-4 | Hardback
Library of Congress Control Number: 2024902256

PRINTED IN THE UNITED STATES OF AMERICA

First Printing 2024

www.jmceli.com

For Georgia.

Acknowledgements

This book was a passion project of mine born out of the love I got from "The Unlife of Lisa Cooper." As a new indie author, I was absolutely humbled and moved by the love and support I got for Lisa. I was inspired to write more, but not only the sequel to "Unlife" but MORE content in general. "The Vampires of 1863" was born of a passion fueled by wonderful readers who inspired me to define more of Lisa's world and history. I must thank all my readers, from the ones who've read Lisa's stories from the beginning to the new readers checking things out for the first time. Thank you! A very special thank you and shout out goes out to my front-line reader, sanity checker, spelling and grammar quality control maven, my wife, Georgia. I want to thank my parents who have been so wonderful and supportive during my writing path. Thank you all so much.

Author Notes

The Vampires of 1863 was originally published in a serial format, with one or more episodes released per week from March 2023 through July 2023. What you are reading is the anthology of that series. Instead of chapters, there are episodes, and they are presented as they were in their original publication, albeit with some grammatical corrections.

I thought it was worth mentioning in case you noticed you were being reminded of details so soon after the details appeared in a previous episode. Originally, this was done to refresh the reader's mind on certain story events since it was often a week or more for a reader to grab the next episode after reading the previous one. I wanted to keep the integrity of the original series, so I left the "reminder prose" alone.

You may also notice that Siobhan speaks with an Irish accent. For readability, I tried not to be too heavy-handed with it. As such, you'll see her say things like "I put on me dress." It isn't that she's talking like a cave-person.

I hope you enjoy Siobhan's adventure. Thanks for Reading!

Episode One

Vengeance

The *India House Tavern* had nothing to do with India.

It faced the harbour on India street, adjacent to the India Warf. I was never sure how these places got their names. India was thousands of miles away from Boston.

The door to the tavern swung open, letting the once-muffled music spill out into the night air in all its drunken, sloppy glory. Not a single whistle nor fiddle was amongst the ensemble.

Noise.

Me quarry stumbled out and onto the street.

I didn't know his name. I just knew he was one of them. The *Know Nothings*.

I waited a moment in case any of his fellows joined him. Earlier, I'd seen a few others leave the tavern in groups. Too risky. I needed one alone.

"You drunken bastards!" the man laughed to himself. "See you tomorrow!"

He waved to an unseen crowd behind a door he'd staggered thirty paces from.

Drunk and alone. Me lucky night.

I tailed him. I didn't want to be too obvious. At one in the morning, the streets were empty, save for us. And he was too pissed to notice me.

He turned onto Milk Street. The long street ran perpendicular to the harbour and pierced well into downtown. It didn't matter. He'd never make it to Broad Street.

I rounded the corner behind him. Flanked by brick buildings on either side, the shadows blotted out the moonlight, bathing us in darkness.

"Nice night," I said.

The man stopped and turned. He squinted at me, as if narrowing his eyes would help him see through his drunken stupor. "What?"

"Nice. Night."

I moved closer.

"You Irish?" He seemed confused.

His eyes bounced up and down, taking me in. I may have spoken like an Irishwoman, but I didn't dress like one. Draped in one of the finest dresses Boston could offer, I looked nothing like a fresh-off-the-boat guttersnipe.

"You lost?" It was more of a jeer than a question of concern.

"No."

"Fucking Irish cow. Yes, you are. They got you all dressed up, eh? But you still talk like them. Bet you stink like them."

"Come closer and find out."

"What are you, some kind of Irish *fancy girl*? You lot turning tricks in the streets now?" he slurred.

"You're one of the Know Nothings."

He smirked, glassy-eyed. "I don't know what you're talking about."

"Interesting tactic you boys have. Playing dumb. You know it just makes you look like an idiot."

He stumbled towards me. "Someone ought to mind that mouth of yours."

The anticipation of the evening had led to this moment. The fool was about to walk right into striking distance of his own accord. Me heart beat faster. A smile spread across me face.

I was going to enjoy this.

He stopped just short of me reach. His eyes fell to me dress. "What are you, rich?"

I'd purchased me dress in Back Bay. Never in me life did I ever imagine I could afford such a thing, and the dress I had on was merely one of the ones I set aside for hunting.

Confusion washed over his face.

Perhaps I played this wrong. I wasn't hunting to feed, I was hunting for vengeance. And looking like someone from downtown instead of the North End, he seemed to consider me in a new light.

I made a note of that. Next time I hunted to throw someone a beating, I'd have to do it in simpler clothes.

"What's the matter? Not so brave when you don't have your boys with you, hm?" I figured I'd lure him another way.

"Huh?"

"You and your Know Nothing friends. Ganging up on lone Irishmen. Six on one in some cases."

His eyes fell to me dress again as he considered me. "Fuck off." He turned and started walking away.

Oh, the hell with this.

In a heartbeat, I closed the distance between us and grabbed the collar of his jacket. I jerked him backwards and behind me.

He cried out in alarm. I whirled around and punched him square in the face.

His nose collapsed with a sickening crunch. Blood splattered from his nostrils and bathed his mouth and chin.

"Ugh! You bitch! My nose!" One hand cradled his pulverized nose. His other hand lashed out and grabbed for me.

I caught his hand with a pedestrian amount of effort. I crushed it within me grasp. Bones cracked between me fingers, and the man screamed out in pain.

I grabbed his jaw. "Shut up, or I'll bust your jaw next. You won't be able to eat solid food for the rest of your life."

He whimpered. "What are you?"

"No one would believe you if I told you." I leapt on him.

I may as well feed on the bastard while I have him.

We tumbled to the ground, and I sank me fangs into him. I covered his mouth with me hand.

Beer-soaked blood hit me tongue. Bitter. As if the copper taste wasn't bad enough.

I pulled back after half a pint. "You're going to stay away from the Irish, you hear me? You and your little friends. You get me?"

He nodded emphatically.

"Good." I resumed me dinner.

The next moment, I found meself tossed aside from behind. I tumbled across the cobblestone and clambered to me feet. Someone was about to get a mouthful of broken teeth.

"Mind yourself, Siobhan," William said.

I was face to face with me creator.

Bullocks.

I straightened and brushed the dirt from me dress. "I was merely hunting."

"Oh, I can see that. Making all sorts of noise in the middle of Milk Street. Did you even charm him?"

"The feeding was an afterthought. I got caught up in teaching him a lesson." I tried to affect a demure tone. I knew I was in trouble.

"Teaching him a..." William couldn't finish the sentence. He glowered at me.

"He's a Know Nothing! And besides, it's one o'clock in the morning. The streets are empty. The city's asleep."

"Or they were until your racket," William growled. "Do you know how dangerous it is to leave them uncharmed? Showing them what we are?"

"You're Irish too," I offered. It was a weak defense. William never had to deal with what normal Irish folk dealt with. He was third generation. He lived downtown. He didn't have our accent.

"I am more than Irish. And so are you. You cling too much to your petty mortal peeves. These men are insignificant. You're letting the trivial matters of your former life cloud your judgement. We talked about this."

Me so-called former life was only three years ago, and I couldn't tell him the truth. I couldn't tell him why I was hunting Know Nothings.

I bowed me head. "I'm sorry."

Me victim had gotten to his feet. He turned, about to make a break for it.

William was on him before I could blink. Not even a blur. Before I could protest, the man's head spun nearly backwards, swiveled on a shattered neck.

William dropped the dead body on the street.

"Why!" I shouted.

His eyes were baleful. "When we do not charm the ones we partake of, we leave them to retain a clear mind of what happened. They talk. They spin stories. There are still places in Europe where those stories are alive and well. But here in the new world? They are myths, and we would do well to keep it that way."

"But you killed him. You could have charmed him."

"I'm surprised you care." He shrugged. "I am not taking chances. Lest you get paid a visit by Tailcoat Jack."

A shiver went up me spine at his name.

Tailcoat Jack. The enforcer of the lord of the New England bleed, Don Esteban Santiago.

"So, we just leave him in the street?" I asked. "We can't exactly call in goblins to magic all this away, and I'm not carrying—"

William put up a hand.

"We leave him here," he said. "The mortals will come up with their own cause of death. Maybe he fell off a horse or was struck by a cart. There is nothing here that links his death to us."

William cast a look at the crumpled stiff at his feet. "But we should go."

"Where?"

William frowned. "I was going to drop you off at the house, but I think you'll need a chaperone tonight."

"I don't need a chaperone. And where are you going?"

"I have a meeting with Ivan. Not your concern." William began walking back toward the India Tavern. I followed behind him, pulling up the hem of me dress.

"I don't need a chaperone," I protested.

"You're acting like a *páiste*. I thought you were old enough to hunt on your own. Maybe I was mistaken."

"So, you'll have Fiddlehead mind me while you're away?"

"No. We're not going home. I'm taking you to Nigel's."

"Nigel's?" That threw me for a loop.

Fiddlehead held the door to William's carriage for us. Me creator's servant was dressed in styles twenty years out of date, but no less dapper. His long tailcoat was embroidered with gold thread and bulky white cuffs peaked out from underneath the sleeves. He wore buckled shoes and a brimmed hat accented with a large floppy feather.

Me eyes allowed me to see through Fiddlehead's glamour, of course. In truth, the goblin was only about three feet tall, and his yellowish skin was covered in knobs and unsightly blemishes. He wasn't much to look at, Fiddlehead, but he and I got on just fine.

"Thanks, Fiddlehead," I said.

"Evenin' Ms. Siobhan. Bashin' heads tonight?"

"That'll do, Fiddlehead. Drive us to Nigel Brigham's," said William.

"Yes, sir."

The little goblin ran off and took the reins while William and I climbed into the carriage.

William's carriage was luxury on wheels. The seats alone were nicer than anything me family had to sit on back home. Leather, stuffed with cotton, and threaded up just as fine as Fiddlehead's coat. The wood was dark and smooth, with swirling designs carved into its interior moulding. The wee windows even had curtains.

Normally, I loved riding in the beautiful coach, but I was too agitated to enjoy it. It wasn't like I was going to sneak out and beat up another Know Nothing. I didn't need a chaperone.

The carriage rolled to life in a lurch, and we were off.

Nigel lived on Tremont Street near the Common. It was a quick drive to get there from where we were. For that, I was thankful. We rode in silence for the short drive. William was still fuming.

We stepped out of the carriage at the front steps. The two-story red-brick house was accented by larger, white bricks that ran up its length, framing the exterior walls. Additional white masonry framed the doorway and windows. It reminded me of something that was built for some founding father in the late seventeen hundreds, but I noticed an engraved cornerstone by the first step that read *1853*.

William rapped on the door.

I braced meself. This whole affair was going to be humiliating.

Oh, hi Nigel. Just dropping off me wee páiste, *who can't be let alone for five minutes lest she be bashing heads on the east side.*

After a moment, Nigel responded, looking surprised. No, not surprised. Worried. Guilty.

"Um... Mister Donovan. What a surprise," Nigel sputtered.

"Nigel!" William affected a smile. "I need to impose on you for a few hours, do you mind?"

"Er..." Nigel looked over his shoulder.

"May we come in?" William didn't wait for an answer. He brushed past Nigel, and I followed in behind him.

Nigel's house reminded me a lot of William's. The furniture was an ensemble of chairs, sofas, desks, and tables that were carved in twisted shapes from dark wood and affixed with poofy cushions upon their seats, backs, and armrests. I fancied such things in the palace of the Queen. Wallpaper adorned the walls up to chair rails that bisected their width. Within their lower half, dark wooden panels ran their length.

It was ornate and luxurious, but so very dreary. It was dark. And in the night, with the curtains drawn, the colourless furniture and walls offered no vibrance to the room.

Nigel crossed out of the foyer and lit a kerosene lamp in the parlour. I followed him inside.

The light didn't do much to bring any cheer to the room.

"Nigel, you know my scion, Siobhan McQueeney?"

Of course, he did. His creator was Ivan MacAlistair, William's ally within the bleed. Nigel and I were often put together; attending the same functions, meetings, and other nonsense with our creators.

"Of course," Nigel smiled. "How do you do, Siobhan?"

"I am well, thank you." I did me best to hide me irritation with the situation. I still had me manners.

He took me hand and kissed it.

I grinned at the display. The git.

"Excellent." William proclaimed. "Nigel, I need to attend a meeting with your creator for a few hours. Would you mind after Siobhan? She's been feeling a little... high spirited this evening."

I glowered at William.

"A few hours?" Nigel asked.

"It won't be a problem?" William asked. There was a thin veil of danger in his tone.

"No. No, sir. Happy to help."

"Good." William placed a gentle hand on me shoulder. "I brought you here not to be cruel, but so you would have someone to enjoy the evening with while I attended to some business. Relax. Socialize. Have fun." He smiled at me.

"Yes, William."

"Nigel." William held out his hand.

Nigel shook it. "Mister Donovan. Don't worry, she's in good hands."

A few more smiles all around, and me creator was out the door.

I folded me arms and flashed Nigel a look.

"What?"

"I can't believe he introduced us. That's three times he's done that."

"It's just good manners, like an announcement." Nigel grinned.

"I see you played the part of the gentlemen meeting the lady and kissing me hand."

Nigel looked over his shoulder again. His nervous expression returned.

"What is it?"

"Tonight isn't a good night for me," he said.

"Perfect." I shrugged. "No offense, it's nice to see you and all, but after the night I had, I think I'd rather be alone. Tell William I grew bored and went out. I'll be home before sunrise."

I moved to the door.

Nigel grabbed me shoulder and held me fast. "I'm afraid I can't let you do that, Siobhan."

Nigel's Secret

NIGEL'S HAND RESTED FIRMLY on me shoulder.

"Just what do you think you're doing?" I asked.

"William made a request of me to keep you here."

I turned to face him, which forced his hand off me shoulder. "So, if I try to leave, you'll stop me?"

Nigel smirked. "It seems like that just happened."

I folded me arms. "Clearly you have something going on. And you don't seem fit for entertaining. So let me be off."

"I would, but I don't want to cross William. Let's just sit. We'll talk and unwind a little." Nigel sat down in one of his grand-looking chairs.

"I don't need to unwind," I snapped at him.

Nigel flashed me a smug look.

"Don't give me that look. I'm perfectly calm!"

He never lost his smirk. He just tilted his head at me.

"Oh, go soak your head."

Nigel finally surrendered to a laugh. "Come on. Sit. Let's while away the time."

Great. Now I have to sit.

I looked around the room for ample places to sit. I appraised Nigel's sofa. The sofa had no arms and featured a sloped back on one side. Perfect for sitting with a bustle. Sitting was a small process unto itself. I never wore bustles before William brought me into this life. I couldn't afford dresses like the ones I owned now.

I backed up slowly until I felt me calf touch the sofa. Then I slowly sat and perched meself on the edge of the couch. The wires of me lobstertail bustle gathered up behind me and formed a small barrier between the small of me back and the back of the sofa.

I was dainty, poised, and annoyed. I hated bustles.

But damn, I looked good in these dresses.

It was awkward. Nigel clearly didn't want company, and I didn't want to be there. Nigel may have been a friend, but tonight was not our night.

Still, I had me manners, so I attempted conversation. I gestured around Nigel's home. "So, all of this is…"

"Mine," Nigel smiled.

"But surely Ivan must have paid for it."

I'd never seen Nigel's house before. I always assumed his wardrobe and other fineries came to him by way of his creator, such as mine did with William. Nigel was turned some years before me, and I had heard he came from humble beginnings.

"When Ivan granted me my independence, he gifted me some seed money, it's true. But most of my wealth is a result of my own investments. I've a lot of money in railroads," Nigel said.

"Oh." I didn't understand a lick of anything when it came to investments.

"William will grant you a bit when you've earned your independence, I'm sure. My advice? Invest it. Railroads, kerosene, things like that. Find something everyone will want or need and put your money in it."

I nodded along like I understood what he meant. *Put money in it*? Like a bank?

Nigel looked away, as if something caught his attention. He didn't say anything. He inclined his head as if trying to listen.

"You seem nervous," I noted.

Nigel sighed. "You shouldn't be here tonight, Siobhan."

"What's going on? Why not?"

Nigel looked beyond the sitting room as if he could see through walls and further into his house. "I'm debating telling you, actually."

I raised me brows at him.

"You and I are the scions of two of the ruling elders of this bleed."

"Obviously. But what does that have to do with anything?" I asked.

"We are the future."

I laughed. Typical Nigel. He had been thrilled when he met me. He went on and on about securing the future and alliances and other nonsense. That was three years ago, and I was too busy being horrified over what had become of me than to have given a damn about his grand designs for the bleed.

"Laugh all you want, but in another hundred years we'll be elders too, and we'll have a seat at the table. The alliances we make now could endure and allow us to mold the future landscape of—"

"What *are* you on about?"

"Power."

I already had me fill of power. I'd gotten more than I'd bargained for already. I contained a laugh as an incredulous smirk spread across me lips.

Nigel smiled at me. "Power enough to secure that vendetta you have against the Know Nothings. That's right, I know all about that. And I'm betting that's why you're here tonight."

Me smirk evaporated. He had me attention.

"Strictly speaking, I could get in a lot of trouble within the bleed for what I'm about to show you. Once I show you, you'll be in this too."

I bristled. "Hold on. I don't even know what this is about. I'm not getting on board with some scheme that could get us both in trouble. You need to give me more details before I agree to anything. Or better yet? Don't. I'm not interested."

"Are you sure? Power enough to stop the Know Nothings once and for all?"

I hesitated. The idea of having the power to rip through Know Nothings was very compelling, but I wasn't about to put meself at odds with the bleed.

"I won't chance crossing Don Esteban. Or the *Scáilic Predominance*," I said.

Nigel waved his hand. "The *Scáilic Predominance* is thousands of miles away in Europe."

"You can't be that dense. There are goblins all over the city and *sidhe* in powerful positions within the bleed. Even the Crocus Tavern is run by a *sidhe*."

"Poppy is hardly an agent of the *Scáilic Predominance*, Siobhan. She's a glorified barmaid. Tailcoat Jack? A thug with no real authority on his own. And goblins?" Nigel laughed, but it was uneasy. "Servants. The true power of the *Scáilic Predominance* is overseas. There are no fae lords here."

I wasn't going to argue with Nigel over it. I may have been a young vampire, a *páiste*, but William educated me well. I knew the fae could travel through Otherworld and cross thousands of miles on Earth in a matter of days.

"Regardless. I won't cross Don Esteban," I said.

He frowned. "Suit yourself. Let me check on something, and when William returns for you, I'll ask you to please urge him away. I really can't receive guests tonight. Especially not William."

I furrowed me brows, partly in defense of me creator and partly over how curt he was being.

Nigel rose from his chair and left the room.

I sat alone, feeling like a fool. I wanted to leave. I was annoyed with Nigel for not being a decent host. We were friends and he'd made me feel like a burden. And I was angry at William. He'd been insensitive. He knew why I hated the Know Nothings. He had no compassion for the fact that I still cared about me roots.

I was still young enough where I hadn't lost me way. Me curse hadn't claimed me yet. And as God is me witness, it never would. Me family will always matter to me, and that was something William would have to deal with.

I heard humming from the other room. A woman's voice.

Humming?

"Shut up you, bitch!" snapped Nigel from the other room.

What a horrible thing to say to a lady! I always took Nigel for a gentleman. Was this Nigel's big secret? Some person? A lover? A *thrall*?

And what was all that talk about power?

The humming continued.

I felt queasy. A nausea suddenly took me. I swallowed involuntarily and bit back the urge to retch.

"Shut UP!" Nigel shouted from the other room. I heard the distinct sound of a slap.

I got to me feet. What the hell was going on?

I left the parlour and entered Nigel's study. Rows of bookshelves consumed the walls. Their dark wood seemed to suck up what little light the kerosene lamps were giving off. Normally, I would have been astonished by the sheer number of books in Nigel's collection, but that wasn't what drew me eye.

A woman, bruised and battered, sat gagged and tied to a chair beside his fireplace. A fire was regaining its life with a fresh log, probably thrown on a moment just before I arrived.

I looked to Nigel, horrified by what I was witnessing. "What are you doing?"

As vampires, I knew we fed off people. I knew we kept thralls. But this poor woman was neither meal nor enthralled.

"You were meant to stay in the sitting room," Nigel said.

"Why is she tied up? What on Earth are you doing?" I was revolted.

"Siobhan, this woman is dangerous. She nearly killed me three nights ago. She's not human. I don't know what she is. She doesn't taste like a fae." He glared at the woman.

"You've been feeding off her? Why not use your gaze on her?"

"I can't. It doesn't work."

I was dubious. This woman was clearly suffering and didn't look dangerous to anyone. "How did she manage to almost kill you?"

"When I tried to charm her, she…"

"What?"

"She started singing." He looked embarrassed over it.

"Singing?" I went from dubious to incredulous.

Nigel gave a nod. "A few seconds later, I was throwing up blood."

"Jesus, Mary, and Joseph." I put me hand over me on stomach. That explained the queasiness. And the humming.

The woman looked up at me. Her eyes were bloodshot and tear-stained. They pleaded to me.

Nigel produced a small leather case from a desk drawer. He pulled out a strange glass cylinder with a needle affixed to it. He set it aside and pulled out a vial of liquid from the same case.

"What's that?"

"This is called a hypodermic needle. Invented by some Scots doctor if you can believe that."

In my village, back in Ireland, doctors were still using goose quills to inject medicine. If you had the money.

"What's in the bottle?"

"Morphine. It'll keep her sedated for a couple of hours. The dose I have to give her is inhuman and costs me a pretty penny. But it keeps her from humming."

"But you drink from her. Wouldn't the morphine—"

"No, I wait until it subsides a little. But she's too dangerous now. I let it go too long. Strange she's not humming. Probably because of you. I bet she's trying to figure you out."

I looked at the woman again. This didn't feel right.

Nigel poked the needle into the vial and pulled back on a hook at the end of the needle's cylinder. The tube filled with liquid.

"So, you just keep her here?"

"Honestly, I would have killed her nights ago, but her blood, Siobhan... oh, her blood." Nigel closed his eyes a moment. "It's potent. It makes me stronger. Faster. But it only lasts a short time."

I wrinkled me nose.

"Siobhan, this... woman. Whatever she is. Her blood is liquid power. So yes, I'm keeping her." Nigel pressed the hook upwards on the cylinder, and a thin spray of liquid shot from the top of the needle. Then he flicked the tube and inspected the result.

"This is barbaric, Nigel. You must see that. You can't blame her for fighting back when you tried to charm her. She's clearly some sort of preternatural being."

The woman's eyes widened at me. I knew that expression.

Hope.

"Have you even been feeding her?"

Nigel shook his head. "No. I can't ungag her. You think her humming is bad. She's only stronger if she can sing."

"She'll starve to death!"

"Eventually, perhaps. But she's stronger than a human. As for me, I'm awaiting some medical equipment. Her suffering will be over soon enough."

"What's that supposed to mean?"

"It means I will soon be in possession of needles like this one that can syphon her blood. I can't keep her indefinitely, but I can take what remains of her."

Me jaw fell open.

I stood in front of him, blocking his path to the woman. "No."

"Siobhan, we are hunters. Sometimes we kill."

"No, we take what is needed, charm, and release."

"You think that's for some humanitarian cause? That's to preserve our secrets. That's so we don't leave a string of bodies in our wake. We are modest in our consumption for *our* needs, not theirs."

I couldn't believe what I was hearing. Nigel was a friend, and only created five years earlier than I. Had he fallen down the dark spiral so quickly? His skin didn't even have a deathly pallor yet.

"She's suffering."

"It's an unfortunate byproduct of the situation. She's too dangerous to release and, if I kill her, her blood is useless to me. Siobhan, you don't understand the *power* of her blood!"

"We're going to cut a deal with her. We release her, and she'll promise not to harm us. She'll agree. I'm sure she doesn't want to die," I said.

"Neither she nor you are in a position to bargain here. We are vampires. We drink blood. And her blood is magic."

"Magic?" I scoffed.

"It's *something*! It's not fae. It's got to be magic. Maybe she's a witch."

"A witch?" I laughed. "Do you even hear yourself? You've become unhinged, you have."

Nigel's face grew dark. "Step out of my way, Siobhan."

The humour drained from me face, and I frowned at him. "No."

Nigel set the needle down gingerly on his desk, then turned back to me. "Then I shall move you."

The Woman In The Chair

I WAS FLABBERGASTED. "I beg your pardon?"

"I said I'll have to move you." Nigel took a step towards me.

I didn't budge. I put me fists at me hips.

"Come on, Siobhan. Enough. Move."

"No."

The bound and gagged woman behind me made a few muffled sounds like *Mm* and *Oo*, but no humming, thank goodness. She was probably trying to get me attention, but I didn't want to turn me back on Nigel.

Nigel stepped up to me, braced me shoulder, and shoved me to one side. "You're being ridiculous."

I stumbled a step, but found me footing. Then I shoved him back. "I'm serious, Nigel. This is monstrous, what you're doing."

That did it. I wounded his pride. The look in his eyes wasn't so much Nigel but a version of him seized by his curse.

He backhanded me and knocked me aside. He gritted his teeth and shut his eyes tight. "Dammit, Siobhan!"

He hit me. I didn't care if his curse compelled him to do it. He *hit* me.

I planted me feet the way me father taught me, then I landed a punch on his jaw. Nigel reeled backward and fell on his ass.

"Aye, me dad taught me how to throw a punch. Don't you ever—"

He leapt on me, eyes wild. Nigel may have been in there somewhere, but for now, his curse had the reins. William had warned me of vampires who couldn't control their temper. Anger was an easy foothold for our curse to latch on to, tempting us with power to fuel vengeance.

And I'd gone and pissed him off.

We both hit the floor. I put up me arms to cover me face. His fist hit me ribs. Lancing pain shot through me middle. To add to the pain, he'd managed to shatter one of the bones in my corset, and it jabbed me side.

"Nigel, stop! Get off!" I yelled.

I rolled on top of him and then hopped off, twisting out of his grasp.

Nigel scrambled to his feet and flew into a flurry of jabs and punches.

He was strong. I evaded what I could, but where I had to block, me forearms bleated in pain.

"You don't understand," Nigel seethed. "She's dangerous. She can't be set free. She can't be saved."

I took a step backwards. "We can talk about this rationally, when you've calmed down. You let your curse—"

"I am in complete control!" he shouted.

The newest log in the fireplace had caught fire enough to shed more light into the room, lending its luminosity to the soft glow of the kerosene lamps. I could see Nigel's face quite clearly.

He'd grown pale. He'd drawn on power in his anger, and the curse had taken its toll.

"What've you done to yourself? You're as pale as a ghost."

Nigel looked at his hands, turning them over and back again. He looked at me and scowled.

"Look what you did!"

"What *I* did? You're the one so pissed off that you let your curse drag you down into this state!" I gestured at him.

I pointed at the woman tied to the chair. "Look at her. Look what you've done to her. It's unconscionable!"

The woman looked up at me, eyes pleading.

"I'm cutting her loose," I said.

"Like hell you are." Nigel marched across the room to the desk. He yanked one of the drawers open and produced a pistol.

He leveled it at the woman. "I'll end this right now."

I stepped in front of him.

"Don't think I won't shoot you, Siobhan."

The woman began to hum. As muffled as it was beneath her gag, her song permeated the room with sweet measures. Yet, as lovely as the melody was, nausea seized me stomach once more.

What in the name of all that was holy? I was trying to help her.

I looked back at her to indicate me dismay. She met me gaze with those same pleading eyes, but this time she chucked her chin in Nigel's direction.

Nigel was getting it worse, clutching his stomach and struggling to keep his pistol trained on us. The woman kept humming.

I charged him, grabbing for his gun.

His hand went up as we both fought for control of the pistol. With our free hands, we pulled and pushed at each other, grabbing onto limbs and clothing like savages.

I got me fingers wrapped around the chamber of his pistol, but Nigel still held the handle firmly. He pulled from me grasp and shoved me away.

Down came the butt of his gun on me head.

I fell down on me ass. Me head was spinning. A loud ringing filled me ears.

"I don't want to hurt you, Siobhan. I'll have enough to explain to William as it is." He brought his gun to bear again. "But she's too dangerous to cut loose. So, you leave me no—"

I reached over and pulled down the woman's gag.

"No!" Nigel shouted.

The woman screamed. A deafening, piercing cry came from her. The inhuman shrill was like daggers in me head. I put me hands over me ears, but it did little to reduce the pain.

Nigel got the worst of it. He was standing in the full path of her screeching. He fired a shot, but it went wild as he was thrown back. Nigel slammed against the wall and crumpled to the floor.

Me ears were ringing to beat hell. I clambered to me feet and kicked the gun away from him. It clattered away and landed on the hearth of the fireplace.

"Jesus, Mary, and Joseph, this got out of hand. You should have let me make a deal with her!"

Nigel could only moan on the floor. He was bleeding out his ears and his right arm was twisted back unnaturally.

"What did you do to him?" I whirled on the woman.

"I think you saw." Her voice was horse. "Get me out of here and I swear I won't hurt you. I'll just leave."

"Or him. You can't harm him either," I said.

"Fine. Just get me out of this damn chair."

I tried to untie the knots, but I couldn't make any sense out of them. After a moment of trying to puzzle them out, I snapped the ropes binding her hands and feet.

"Look out!" the woman shot up out of the chair and shoved me aside.

I stumbled a few steps away and spun to regain me footing. Nigel had gotten up and retrieved his gun.

What came next happened too fast. I couldn't stop it.

The woman screamed again. Nigel was blown backwards once more.

Into the fireplace.

"Bloody Hell! Nigel!" I moved to the hearth.

Nigel's clothes caught fire. He screamed and flailed about, trying to get his hand underneath him to push himself up. His legs kicked and one of his hands slipped off the pile of wood underneath him.

"Take me hand!" I reached for him.

Nigel planted his hands at last and got his legs stable. He launched himself at me. Murder in his eyes.

"I'll kill you!"

Before I could protest, we both tumbled onto the floor. Nigel was still on fire and the stench of burning fabric stung me nostrils.

"Get off me!" I shouted. "We need to put you out."

I was fending Nigel's hands from clasping around me neck.

The woman grabbed Nigel by the coat tails. He clawed at me to keep from being pulled back, but I wouldn't let him gain purchase on me.

Gritting her teeth, the woman dragged Nigel off me.

"Me dress is on fire!" I tried patting the flames, but the fire stung me palms and did little to snuff it out.

Nigel got to his feet and shoved the woman aside. Fire licked up his trousers and scorched his coat. In all his struggling, he'd done nothing to try to subdue his flames.

"Nigel!"

"I'll kill you both! I—" He screamed as the fire climbed along his torso.

The woman broke the chair over Nigel, and he went down in a blazing, caterwauling heap.

Me dress was catching fire. Flames licked at me legs. I rolled, turning meself upon the floor this way and that.

The woman was looming over Nigel, a broken chair leg in her hands.

I kept rolling as the fire singed me shins.

She pulled me upright. "Hold still." The woman patted the hem of me dress and bustle furiously with her own bare hands. "You got most of it."

Burning flesh fouled the air. Nigel's screams had hoarsened into shallow gasps.

Then silence.

I got to me feet.

Nigel was burnt horribly; black and red chars scorched his face. The fire had found its way further along and consumed him.

Yet, he wasn't making a sound. He wasn't moving.

Me eyes fell to the stake embedded in his chest.

"You staked him!"

"He wasn't going to stop coming after us. You stake a vampire and you shut off his powers. He wasn't able to heal when the flames took him."

I went to him and pulled the stake from his chest.

"Nigel!"

"He's dead," the woman said bluntly.

"Oh, my God. We killed him."

"I killed him."

I looked at the woman. Her eyes were bleary. Her face was gaunt from starvation. The corners of her mouth were bruised from the gag. Her wrists were rubbed raw from her bindings.

But she fixed me with a steely gaze. She put a foot behind her and took on a stance that reminded me of the footing me father taught me as to throw a punch from. She took in a deep breath.

I put me hands up. "You're free."

Her shoulders relaxed a bit. She released her breath.

We stared at each other a moment.

I willed meself not to start crying. How did things get so out of hand? Nigel was dead. And I was in a lot of trouble.

"My name is Leucosia. Friends call me Lucy," she said.

What an insane time for an introduction. "Why are you telling me this?"

"Because I owe you. We'll be bonded now, you and I. *The Fates* will remember what you have done for me."

I didn't understand a lick of what she was talking about. All I knew was that she needed to leave before William got back, and I needed to figure out what to do about Nigel.

"I'm Siobhan. But you should go. Me creator will be back, and you can't be here when he returns."

"You don't have to tell me twice. And Siobhan... thank you."

I gave her a weak nod as me eyes lingered over Nigel's body. He didn't look like himself anymore. Me friend was dead.

I don't know how long I sat there, lost and numb. I tried to fathom what had just happened over the course of a few minutes.

Should I hide the body? Run away? Ask William for help?

Oh, God. William. Would he kill me for this? Drag me to Ivan MacAlistair, Nigel's creator?

Me sorrow and regret spun into fear.

I couldn't cover this up. He'd kill me for it.

Time slipped away, and I stewed in me despair until a knock came at the door.

William.

Episode Four

William

"Wɪʟʟɪᴀᴍ." I ɢʀᴇᴇᴛᴇᴅ ᴍᴇ creator at the door.

I could only imagine what I looked like. Hair unkempt. Dress burnt. And the smell.

There was no way to cover up the smell of Nigel's charred remains.

William's nostrils flared. He frowned. "What happened? Where is Nigel?"

"You better come inside."

William followed me in. "What on Earth happened to your dress? Honestly, I leave you alone to keep you out of trouble, and you—"

"Nigel's dead."

William stiffened. He sniffed the air again.

"William, he…"

Me creator didn't listen. He stalked into the other room, presumably following his nose towards the scent of death.

"Jesus Christ." William loomed over Nigel. "What happened!"

I explained everything to him. Me summary of the tragic events came out hurried and anxious. William never looked at me. Throughout the entire story, he stood scowling at Nigel's smoldering body.

When I finished, only a fearful silence remained. I was waiting for him to react. To strike. Perhaps to kill me for what I'd let happen.

"Singing, you said. He feared her singing," he said at last.

"Yes. Even when she hummed it… affected us."

William bent down and picked up a stray piece of rope from the chair Lucy had been bound to. "You broke this?"

"Yes." His sudden focus on the rope confused me.

"Three quarter inch hemp. You're getting stronger."

What was I supposed to say to that? *Thank you*? Why wasn't he screaming at me?

William stood back up. "This will be a problem. Nigel was an idiot. He should have at least gone to Ivan with this, but he got greedy."

"What do we do?"

He looked at me thoughtfully, then he frowned. "Honestly, Siobhan, you probably should have just went along with this little hostage situation and then told either Ivan or myself about it."

"She was starving. He was killing her."

William shook his head. "You're still a *páiste*, Siobhan. Sentimental and burdened by your sense of humanity."

"It's not a burden," I insisted.

"Now is not the time for you to be contrary with me. You exasperated a simple situation that could have been maneuvered to avoid Nigel's death."

"What would Ivan have done with Lucy if I had told him about her?"

"*Lucy*?" William's face darkened. "You're on a first name basis with this creature? A member of our bleed, Ivan's own scion, lays dead at our feet and you're making acquaintance with his killer?"

"Are you going to turn me in?"

William glowered at me, then looked down at Nigel thoughtfully. "I have to."

Fear seized me heart. "What'll happen to me? Don Esteban will—"

"Esteban? No, I won't be turning you into our dear Bleed Lord. Esteban must never know about this. But Ivan? We can't keep this from Ivan. He'll want to learn what happened to his scion and his investigations would reveal us to Esteban."

I furrowed me brow. "But won't Ivan be aggrieved by this? He'll just go to Don Esteban anyway."

"No. I don't think he will. Esteban will hold me accountable as I am your creator, and you are still a *páiste*. Ivan and I have come too far for him to take that risk. He needs me."

"What does that mean?"

"That's none of your concern. For now, you're going to help me clean this place up and find something to put the body into. We'll dump him in the harbor."

It was a morbid and sickening affair.

The cleanup consisted of burning the broken pieces of the chair and ropes in the fireplace. I found a broom and swept up. Parts of the hardwood floor had scorched where Nigel fell. I moved a rug in from the other room to cover it up.

As for Nigel, William crammed him into a trunk we found upstairs. It was horrible. William bent, twisted, and broke Nigel's body so it fit inside. I couldn't look at what had become of him. Charred beyond recognition. Folded up in a box like a broken toy.

Nigel was me friend. Regardless of how far things got out of hand, I was sick over it. William tried to convince me that Lucy's blood must have made him crazy. Like a laudanum addict.

"What now?" I asked.

"We dump him in the harbor. The trunk will sink. I stabbed holes in the bottom."

"We'll simply carry the crate down the street?"

"Don't be ridiculous. We'll put the crate in the carriage and drive down to the water."

"But, Fiddlehead is our driver. The goblins are part of the *Scáilic Predominance*. Won't he say something to Don Esteban?"

He flashed me an annoyed look. "One thing at a time, Siobhan. For now, I want you to get that trunk into the carriage."

There were too many moving parts and variables for me liking, but I inclined me head to me creator. "Yes, William."

I picked up the trunk and carried it to the front door. The musty trunk mingled with the smell of blood and charred flesh. I gagged more than once.

William stepped out into the night air. "Fiddlehead! Fiddlehead! Fiddlehead!"

Fiddlehead, wherever he was, would feel pull of his summon; his name cried three times. Fae always loved things in threes. I never understood why.

A short time later, Fiddlehead pulled the carriage in front of Nigel's house.

He cocked an eye as I loaded the trunk inside.

"That smells like right death, that does," he said.

"Take us to the waterside," said William, offering no explanation to the goblin.

"Pull yourself together, Siobhan," William snarled at me. "You look gaunt. And not in the way belying power."

I frowned at him. I couldn't bloody well articulate how I felt. Fiddlehead would hear. William's driver may have been his servant, but he was on retainer from and answered to the hierarchy of fae.

After a short ride of stomach-churning anxiety, we reached the side of the road overlooking Long Wharf.

Without a word and no ceremony, William grabbed the horrid trunk and climbed out of the carriage. I followed out after him.

"What's this business, eh?" Fiddlehead peered from his driver's roost.

William ignored him. He simply hefted his burden and cast it into the harbour.

The trunk bobbed lazily for a moment before taking on water. It went lopsided, upended, and then slowly sank into the depths.

I felt like we should say something. Some words for Nigel. This was sort of his funeral, after all. But I didn't dare open me mouth.

William glared at me.

I lowered me eyes. "William, I—"

The carriage shook. William had leapt up into the driver's seat and seized Fiddlehead. The little goblin flicked his fingers igniting sulfurous sparks, but it was too late. With a sickening crack, William snapped his neck.

I was horrified. "You killed him!"

"Keep your voice down," he rasped at me. "Of course, I killed him. You said it yourself. He would go talking and asking questions. The last thing we need is fae poking their noses into this. You want Tailcoat Jack to get word of what we've done?"

"No." I was shaking.

"Get into the carriage. We'll talk when we get home."

Fiddlehead's body, clothes and all, faded away in a glow of dust. It reminded me of fireflies. It only lasted a moment or two, but when the glow dissipated, all traces of him were gone.

I gasped. "Where did he go?"

"Otherworld, the faerie realm. Better this way. No body. Now get inside. I won't tell you again."

I climbed into the carriage with a lot of questions, none of which I was particularly keen on asking. *So, Fiddlehead's dead body would just appear somewhere else? Nobody would ask about that?* I knew about Otherworld. Fae traversed to and from there all the time.

William took the reins of the cart, and soon we were on our way.

William and I lived on Congress Street. He had me decked out with me own living quarters all to meself. It was almost like having me own apartment within his building just one floor down from William's.

Many of our mortal neighbors thought we were having some sort of premarital tryst. The spinster and the older gentleman upstairs. Scandalous.

We were home after a few minutes' ride.

"Get out," William barked.

I climbed out of the carriage, trying to keep me mannerisms demure. Perhaps if I looked pitiable, William would go easy on me. Then again, that tactic rarely worked.

Like most of the architecture downtown, William's building was made of brick and had three floors. The interior was brighter than Nigel's, with white panels and moulding and many sconces of kerosene to provide plenty of light.

In a rare moment of sensitivity, William had told me how much he missed the sun. It was why he liked things bright. I'd never forgotten that.

He followed me up to me floor, shutting the door behind us. Me own apartment was bright as well, but scarcely furnished. It was an odd time to think of it, but I thought about getting a few of those ornate, poofy chairs; like the ones Nigel had.

Reality settled back in. William glowered at me. I remembered he said we had to tell Ivan what had happened. Anxiety pulled me out of me brief furniture interlude.

"What do we do about Ivan? Do you think he'll—"

"You impetuous girl! How could you let this happen? Nigel is *dead*! I had to kill a perfectly good driver to cover up your mess!"

There it was. The reaction I had expected. His rage had only been simmering underneath a calm veneer.

"Do you realize how much danger you have put me in? If Ivan decides he is... how did you word it? *Aggrieved*? If he is so aggrieved that he's willing to throw away what he and I have been working toward to see his scion avenged?"

I had no idea what he and Ivan were working towards.

"I told you, it was the woman! I tried to save him!"

"No, you tried to save *her*. That woman was nothing. People die all the time, and we must make hard choices in order to survive."

Barbaric, selfish nonsense. And after three years, I was sick of it. I took a swing at him.

William looked marginally surprised, but he stepped aside and pushed me shoulder, sending me staggering away.

"The guts on you. I still can't tell if you're brave or stupid," he said.

"I'd rather take me lumps than live as the person you want me to be," I spat. I got into a boxer's stance, fists up.

"Hmph. Well, your lumps could very well get you killed." William appraised me stance. "Who taught you that?"

"Me dad."

He frowned. "There is a fire in you, Siobhan. Passion. I want to hone it. I want to shape you into something formidable. I knew it the night you resisted my charming gaze three years ago."

"I'm not some piece of steel you can mold."

William shook his head. "I'm saying that, if you trust me, I will protect you against Ivan. Despite your mistakes. But you need to listen to me and stop being so reckless."

I relaxed and dropped me fists. "Don't seem to have much of a choice."

"No, you don't. Ivan may demand your execution. If I'm going to put my neck on the line for you, I need to know you will never put me in this position again." He took a step towards me.

I made a half-hearted attempt to raise me fists again but let me arms drop. "Fine. Deal."

His expression softened. "We old vampires worry too. Killing a member of our own bleed is a serious offense." He adopted a soft expression.

"But I didn't kill him."

"I don't know that Ivan or Don Esteban will see it that way. Now come." He held his arms outstretched. "Come on."

I gave a wan smile and wandered into his embrace.

William held me close, and I put me arms around him.

I finally felt safe. The horrors of the night melted away within his hold.

"Now go and get cleaned up. The sun will be up soon, and I want to get an early start tomorrow night."

I pulled back and gave him a quizzical look.

To answer me unasked question, William supplied, "We need to see Ivan."

So much for feeling safe.

Episode Five

The Wheelock Sword

Ivan's house was older than William's. Based on the crown moulding, I placed it somewhere in the late seventeen hundreds.

The walls in the sitting room were stenciled in patterns likely from the original paints used decades ago. Drab orange flowers and green vines were plastered from floor to ceiling. The furniture looked antiquated. The simple ladder-back style of the chairs and sturdy wooden frame of the sofa belied their age. The goblins kept things dusted and neat, but I wondered if Ivan even used this room.

Me musings offered little comfort as me stomach rolled in knots.

In the drawing room, behind closed doors, William and Ivan were talking about Nigel's death. They had been shouting not too long ago, but now I scarcely heard a whisper.

I'd heard very clearly that Ivan wanted me head for this.

Part of me wanted to flee into the night, but William had told me whatever happens, he would protect me. And I believed that.

Me stomach, however, still tightened in unconvinced coils.

The double doors opened with a slow, mournful creak. William stepped through first, arms wide pushing the doors aside. Ivan followed. William looked grim. Ivan wore a scowl that only darkened when he laid his eyes upon me.

Me heart filled with lead.

William shook his head and glanced at Ivan. He frowned when he finally spoke. "We have reached an agreement."

"Are you going to kill me?" I asked.

"No." William shook his head. "But you are indebted to Ivan."

Me mind raced. I wished he'd just tell me. I jumped to the next suspicion. "I'll not be staying with you then?"

"No, you'll still stay with me." William shook his head again. Whatever it was, he struggled with it.

"Tell me," I insisted.

Ivan, at last, cracked a hint of a smile. A sneer, really.

William's face darkened. "Ivan wants you to retrieve something for him. He wants to you steal the Wheelock Sword."

I drew a blank. "What is it?"

"It's a sword, held by a private collector, here in town." William opened his mouth to say more but closed it again.

"You want me to break into someone's house and steal something." The declaration was as absurd as the tone I gave it.

William nodded.

"And if I refuse?" I think I already knew the answer, but I mustered the courage to ask anyway.

Ivan stepped forward. "Then we will bind you, stake you, and leave you for the sun."

William held up a hand to Ivan. "She'll do it. Just give us time. We need a plan."

"I want that sword," Ivan said.

"And you'll get it. But if she fails, you get nothing. We need a few nights to plan. Plus, we agreed on sending Siobhan to Crocus to ask around," retorted William.

Crocus? Why was I being sent to Crocus?

"Fine. I'll give you two nights." Ivan turned his glare to William. "We're running out of time as it is."

William was between drivers, so we walked home from Ivan's house. Me creator remained quiet and brooding.

"So, how much shit am I in?" I asked. I was afraid of the answer, but I couldn't stand the silence any longer.

William huffed and looked at me. "The sword, the Wheelock sword, is in the possession of Thomas Coffin Amory. Recently appointed Charmain of the Board of Aldermen, former state legislator, and all-around *Boston Brahmin.*"

"Boston Brahmin?" I scrunched me nose in perplexity.

"A cheeky euphemism for the city's elite caste, as it were."

"So, Ivan expects me to break into a senator's house and steal a sword? He's mad."

"We are not in a position to refuse. Ivan is livid over the death of Nigel. He wanted to see you dead tonight. This was the best compromise I could arrange."

"I'm not a bloody burglar. I don't know the first thinking about skulking around."

"We'll take time to plan. But first, we need to do some damage control. I need you to go to the Crocus Tavern and do a little investigating."

"The Crocus Tavern?" I scrunched me nose again, this time in disgust.

"Fiddlehead often went there to drink whiskey with other goblins after he'd dropped me off. I had to summon him, which suggests he was out and away. If he was at the tavern, I want to know if he mentioned us being at Nigel's. We need to know whom he may have told."

"You want me to interrogate goblins?"

"Nothing so direct. Be subtle. The goblins will want to serve you while you're there. Strike up a conversation. See what you can find."

"Alright." I wasn't comfortable with the plan.

"We need to know if Fiddlehead told anyone we were at Nigel's. If that got out, we could have a real problem. I can't be seen hobnobbing with goblins, but a *páiste* like you won't raise any suspicions. This is important, Siobhan."

I shrugged a shoulder. "Very well. I'll do me best."

He pointed in the direction of the tavern. "Dig around then return straight home. We'll discuss what you find out and see if we need to plug up any loose ends. Then we'll devise a plan for the sword."

I furrowed me brow. I didn't like the sound of *plug up loose ends*. I wasn't keen on seeing anyone killed: human, goblin, or otherwise.

"I'll need the password to gain entrance," I reminded him.

"Sugarplums," William supplied.

"*Sugarplums?*"

"It changes every night."

"How do you find out what it's changed to?"

"Telegraph." He grinned.

I shook me head. I couldn't keep track of all the new-fangled technology.

"Go. See what you can find out." William all but shooed me away.

I simply gave William a quick inclination of me chin and set out into the night.

I hated the Crocus Tavern.

It always made me uncomfortable. Whether it was the blood-soaked dalliances of morally vacant vampires or that the tavern was run by a member of the *Scáilic Predominance*. Being inside made me skin crawl and put me on edge.

The Crocus Tavern was a place where vampires could do all the horrible things we do in shadows out in the open.

"Password?"

The gravelly voice came from a door slat about three feet off the ground.

I stooped down a little to answer. "Sugarplums."

The metal slat slammed with a clank and the door swung open. A goblin doorman stared up at me.

Me eyes could see through his glamour, but to a mortal, he would have appeared as a normal sized human. The goblin was dressed in embroidered finery with ridiculously wide lapels on his jacket and coattails that nearly touched the floor. His buckle shoes gave way to stockings and knickers. The lavish outfit was a stark contrast to his dreadful features. The goblin had a sharp, curved nose, ears like cabbage leaves, and blotchy orange skin.

I stepped inside. Piano music filled the room. Someone was playing Beethoven. The classy music was a civilized façade draped over the decadence of the tavern.

"Enjoy your time here, lass. Madame Poppy welcomes you," the little goblin said.

Madame Poppy was a *sidhe*, a fae noble. I'd seen her once. She was stunning beyond compare, with milk-white skin and long braids of silver hair. But it was her eyes that I remembered most of all. They were green, but nothing like mine. Her eyes were like iridescent emeralds that seemed to cast their own light. All the men fawned over her. And a few of the women.

"Thank you," I replied.

"Don't look so stiff. You're among friends here. You got your feeding card?"

"Actually, I was wondering if Fiddlehead had been here last night."

"Fiddlehead? I don't know. Memory's a little cloudy." The goblin grinned at me.

I frowned. "Would a dollar jar that head of yours?"

The little orange creep scoffed. "I'm insulted you didn't start at two. But I don't want your *money*."

I bristled. Goblins were fae, and like all fae, they used vampire blood to keep from being pulled back to Otherworld. Something about the curse in our blood kept fae tethered to Earth.

I took a quick scan around the tavern. There were at least a dozen goblin servants running around. If this little bastard wanted a bit of me blood, then it stood to reason they all would. I'd be drained dry.

I looked at the goblin plainly, controlling me frustration. "Four dollars."

The goblin sputtered. Money wasn't useless to fae. They were living in the city, after all, and goblins were still goblins. They loved their gold and shiny things. Four dollars was probably about what he was making in a week.

"You have deal," he said at last. "Money first."

I dug through the openings of me skirt and into the pockets tied around me waist. I counted out some ones and various coins. This was going to be an expensive night.

The diminutive doorman counted his spoils. "Yea, I saw Fiddlehead come in. He was chatting with Muleskinner." He pointed across the way to a goblin carrying a tray with copper cups. The little waiter weaved through the crowd, delivering his bloody libations.

"Ta," I said, and set off.

Once I stepped into the proper area of the tavern and made me way towards the throng of people Muleskinner traversed, I was starkly reminded of why I loathed coming here.

Mortals in white nightgowns flitted through the room. Men and women scratched notches on feeding cards and thrust their wrists under the noses of their vampire patrons.

It reminded me of sheep offering themselves to wolves. Many of the gowns were stained with blood.

Out in the open, sitting on barstools and sofas, vampires fed freely from their mortal vessels. A few drank from cups served by the goblins, but the true appeal of the Crocus Tavern was what they called *live feeding*.

I didn't just hate the practice of live feeding. I hated how it made me feel.

Conflicted.

The smell of blood permeated the entire room and me curse rose from its depths. A subtle haze settled over me mind. I concentrated on the moment, and tried to stay grounded, but the scent of precious vitae overwhelmed me senses.

A man leaned against the wall across the room. His white gown was stained in splotches of blood. He was like a wallflower looking for someone to dance with, pen in hand and hopeful to notch someone's feeding card.

The sight of his bloody gown sent a longing through me. Me stomach felt hollow. Me fangs elongated.

I glided across the room towards him. He smiled at me.

Me eyes locked onto his. I was walking through a room thick with blood saturated air. The scent of it hung like a fog, and it was all I could do not to leap upon the man.

The haze around me mind thickened. I scarcely registered him offering a salutation. I didn't reply. I couldn't find the words.

Me charming gaze hadn't quite landed. It was a skill I was still learning to master.

No matter. In Crocus, the vessels didn't need to be charmed. I closed the distance between us.

The man backed up against the wall, but he had nowhere to go. He was saying something. Protesting. Fear consumed his eyes.

He made a move to leave. I grabbed his wrist and pulled him back. I pushed him against the wall.

I pressed me body against his, pinning him to the wall. He was shouting now, but through me haze I couldn't make out what he was saying. I didn't care.

I pulled his head down to expose his neck.

Me conflict flickered. Through the clouds, the small voice of me conscience bade me to stop. It was a voice me curse had shoved down, but it struggled to be heard.

Feeding without a card was considered stealing.

Stealing from Madame Poppy.

A *sidhe* noble of the *Scáilic Predominance.*

The man looked at me, terror in his eyes. "Please. Let me go."

Blood's copper aroma wafted from the stains of his gown and tickled me nostrils. I closed me eyes and took a deep inhale through me nose. The scent of life itself.

"Please...," he pleaded.

The haze took me once more. Nothing else mattered.

He screamed as me fangs pierced his skin.

Episode Six

Losing Control

THE MAN IN ME arms struggled as I drank. His strength was no match for mine.

Me mind was a blur, clouded by the scent of blood.

Had the music stopped?

Were people staring at me?

A firm hand grabbed me shoulder. I fought against it as it pulled me back. Whoever it was, I couldn't match his strength. I let go of me quarry and turned to face the interloper.

I grabbed his lapels and pushed him. He didn't budge.

The newcomer shoved me back. Through me haze, I vaguely made out what he was saying. He was telling people to settle down. Saying I was only a *páiste*.

He grabbed me shoulders. He shook me once, then twice.

"Her name is Siobhan," came a voice from the crowd.

Hearing me name was sobering, grabbing me attention and making me pause.

What was I doing?

I looked upon at the man who intervened upon me feeding. He was dressed in the garb of a Boston elite. He was clean shaven, conventionally handsome, with dark hair, deep brown eyes, and a lean build. He was smirking at me.

It annoyed me.

The man I had been feeding on fled the scene. What had I done?

Guilt washed over me as reality settled in. I'd lost control.

"I'm sorry," I muttered.

"You're goin' tae be sorry," came a voice beside me.

Madam Poppy was a stunning sight to behold. Her beauty was inhuman, almost unsettling. Her porcelain features were devoid of any natural crease or wrinkle. Her green eyes were bright and vibrant, nearly giving off light of their own. She was shorter than me, slim and with a dress that cinched her waist and sported a large bustle.

But the woman had other unearthly features marking her as one of the fae nobles. Her hair was white like silver, her ears bore slight points, and the most telltale sign of all: long, curved goat-like horns sprouted from her head.

Like all *sidhe*, her alien appearance was hidden behind her glamour, but me eyes could penetrate her illusions.

She frowned at me, and I realized I was staring.

"You'll have to excuse her, Madam," the interloper said. "She's young. I'll see to it that it's straightened out."

Madam Poppy shifted her eyes from me to the man. She stared at him a moment. "Live feedin's are one thing, but Ah'll nae have this tavern turned intae a free-for-ahll."

"Of course not," the man said. "Here." He fished inside of his jacket and pulled out some money. "This ought to cover the drink."

Me head was still reeling. Me actions had started to settle in. I'd attacked that poor man and now I was getting the kind of attention from Madam Poppy that no one wanted. And who was this person forking out his own money to help me?

The *sidhe* took the bills and folded them neatly into her palm. "Keep the *páiste* on a short leash. Ah'll nae have this conversation with you or her again."

With that, the proprietor of the Crocus Tavern glided away and on to other business.

"Thank you," I said meekly.

The man grinned at me. "You can owe me. Who is your creator? Is he not here?"

"William Donovan. And no, I came here for a drink."

"Well, you certainly got your drink." He smirked at me.

I frowned.

"Apologies. How crass of me. You're William's scion? Yes, that's right. The Irish girl. Shevon, isn't it?"

I gave a slow nod. His pronunciation was close enough.

He held out a hand. "Richard Davenport."

I took it. It was chill to the touch.

Richard lifted me hand and kissed the back of it. "Your hand is still warm. Ah, the blessings of youth. What's it been, three years? And you still have warm skin? Impressive."

"How did you make her back off so quickly? I'd heard stories of how scary she can be."

"Poppy?" Richard waved it off. "I'm the scion of Don Esteban Santiago. If I say something is handled, it's handled."

Whatever lingering haze fogging me mind was dashed in one sobering moment. I was speaking to the scion of the Lord of the New England bleed.

Things were way out of hand. All I wanted to do was leave.

But first, I needed to ask a few questions of Muleskinner. There were many goblins milling around the room, but none of them were him.

Richard followed me gaze about the room.

"Looking for someone?" He grinned.

I smiled politely. "Mister Davenport, thank you for your assistance. Me creator is expecting me, and I need to wrap up some things here."

"That sounds... intriguing. What, pray tell, are you looking to *wrap up*? Anything I can help with?"

His smile wasn't sincere. I needed to get away from this man.

"Richard!" A boisterous call came from across the room.

A man approached us, just as pale as Richard.

This man's ensemble was different than Richard's, though equally lavish. His coat had wide lapels and thin cuffs. Around his neck was a cravat tied into a floppy bow. The man's waistcoat had pinstripes on it, which seemed outrageous to me.

The man looked from Richard, to me, and then back to Richard before extending a hand to him.

"Henry," Richard said.

"Am I too late? The doorman said there was a bit of a commotion."

"Nothing out of the usual. Henry Thatcher, allow me to introduce Shevon...." He looked at me.

"McQueeney," I supplied.

"Shevon McQueeney. William's scion."

Henry looked me up and down, appraisingly. I didn't care for it.

"Ah, yes," Henry said. "I've heard of you. Irish."

"Is that a problem?" I asked.

He hesitated before taking me hand and raising it to his lips. "Of course not."

Richard was grinning like a fool unable to keep a joke to himself. I looked at him curiously. He flashed his teeth. "Henry is a member of the American Party."

The American Party? I snatched me hand from Henry's. "A fecking Know Nothing?"

Richard and Henry both laughed. "She's feisty, this one," said Richard.

"You'll have to excuse Richard. He's always stirring the pot. It's been a long time since I cared about mortal politics," said Henry.

I glared at him, nonetheless.

Henry gave an amused smile. "My political affiliations are a relic of my mortal life. Whatever grievances I had with the Irish have fallen away to the pursuit of much more delightful things."

"Everyone bleeds red," Richard added with a grin.

I rolled me eyes. I had no taste for this sort of humour.

I gave Henry a tight smile. "It was nice to meet you," I said curtly.

"Richard, thank you again, but I must away."

"No, don't go," Henry implored. "I have affronted you. The truth is, I'm more surprised than anything. I didn't think there were any Irish vampires."

"What's that supposed to mean?"

Henry smiled. "There is a lot of conjecture surrounding it, but tales say all the vampires of Ireland have either been destroyed or taken to ground. And, well, no one is making any more of them."

I frowned. I'd heard the so-called *conjecture*. Inferior stock. Undesirable scions. The list went on. I knew the stories. Me creator taught me well.

"Any educated among us know the truth," I said.

"Oh?" Henry leaned forward. "What is the truth?"

"When the old gods of Ireland realized their folly, they set the fae upon the vampires. The vampires fled Ireland and traveled deeper and eastward into Europe. The fae chased them down and brought them to heel."

Henry smirked. "You're talking about the origins of the *Scáilíc Predominance*. You're pretty bold to speak so brazen of the *Tuatha Dé Danann*. Especially in a place like this."

I shrugged.

He let out a laugh. "Oh, I like you, Miss McQueeney. You have... spirit."

Richard looked between Henry and me expectantly.

For a moment, I almost considered giving Henry the benefit of the doubt. Then I saw it.

His smile never reached his eyes.

"There now," announced Richard. "All friendly. But, alas, my hands are empty and I'm standing in the middle of a tavern. Shevon, care for a goblet? My treat."

Me talking to Muleskinner was a bust. I wanted to leave, but me brief dalliance upon that poor man had left me wanting more. Drinking from a proper vessel would be a nice respite from sucking on someone's neck like an animal. I had to admit the tavern had its appeal, unruly debauchery aside.

"Perhaps one drink," I conceded.

Richard's gaze fell behind me. "Oh, lovely. Look who's come to join the party."

I turned around.

Through his glamour I saw a thin male *sidhe* of medium height. He walked with a fancy looking cane, though he seemed to have no practical need for it. His coat was cut above the waist in the front and fell into long tails in the back. A bright blue vest and tie completed the ostentatious ensemble.

He was handsome in an almost luminous way. His long silver hair was pulled back into a ponytail. His horns were polished smooth and shiny. His smile was sinister, attached to baleful eyes.

"Is that—" I'd only heard stories.

"Tailcoat Jack," Richard supplied.

The lanky fae noble sidled up to our small group. "And what are we talkin' about on this *fine* evenin'?"

Henry looked confused and guarded.

Richard remained composed. "Nothing special. We were just about to get a goblet."

Jack grabbed me arm. "Ye'll nae mind if Ah borrow the *páiste*?"

"Hey!" I protested. His grip squeezed like a vice.

Richard frowned. "I'm sure she's of no interest to you, Jack. It was a small altercation, and it's settled."

Jack sneered at Richard. "Ah dinnae care about some *bloodboy*. Ah've come tae have a pleasant conversation with this wee lass."

"I'm sure there's a misunderstanding," Richard persisted.

"Nae, there isnae. Ye'll want none of me, Richard Davenport. I dinnae care whose scion ye be."

Richard stiffened.

Me stomach turned sour. What did *Tailcoat Jack* want with me?

Me would-be protector and the *sidhe* stared at each other a moment before Jack huffed and pulled me away. He led me to the far side of the room.

His hold on me arm hurt, but I was too frightened to protest.

Jack rounded me back against a wall and released his hold on me. "The doorman says you've been asking questions about Fiddlehead."

"He's me creator's driver," I said. I tried to keep me tone calm.

"I ken who he is!" Jack snapped. "Why would ye need to ask about him? Why nae ask him yourself?"

I shook me head. "No reason, just curious about what he talks about when he's here."

"Oh! Interested in goblin gossip, are we?" He sneered. "It's my job to sniff out suspicious things, and you reek of suspicion. Why would a *páiste* be pokin' her nose around the likes of goblin chatter?"

"Nothing. No reason. I told you, I was just curious." I frowned at him. "I didn't do anything wrong."

"*The lady doth protest too much, methinks.*" He grinned.

I frowned, but I didn't bite on his *Hamlet* reference.

"No, wee *páiste*, nothing wrong with poking around goblin business, but it certainly has my attention. Ah'll have my eye on ye."

He grabbed me chin. Cold fingers dug into me cheeks.

Why was his hand so cold?

He gazed into me eyes. "Ah love findin' guilty vampires. The fear. It makes the blood so delicious."

"I didn't do anything wrong," me voice came out quivering.

"We'll see. Muleskinner, was it? Ah'll speak to him next. Find out what you were so keen on learnin'. Then Ah'll have a talk with Fiddlehead. See what he was to say. Then we'll see what you're up to, wee *páiste*."

Me blood ran cold.

Family Time

I GOT UP THE next evening as the last rays of the sun receded over the horizon. I waited in the greeting room until the shadows grew long enough to consume the floor and walls, then I slipped out into the night.

William would still be asleep for another hour or so. At his age, even the twilight of dusk was deadly. But for my youth, dusk was still bearable. Me curse had yet to take that from me.

It was just as well. William was still upset over what happened last night.

I'd told him about what happened in the Crocus Tavern and how Tailcoat jack was sniffing around. He tried not to be angry at me, but tethered to the root of the problem as I was, his aggravation still permeated through all his attempts at calm.

Tonight was not a night I wanted to linger around the house waiting for him to get up.

He was going to see Ivan tonight and warned me that Ivan would have to reveal Nigel's murder to Don Esteban. He'd blame everything on Lucy, the *entity* that I'd rescued and who had killed Nigel.

She would now have the bleed hunting her, and I would be further in Ivan's debt for all his inconvenience.

I had several blocks to travel before the North End. I stewed over all the misfortune swirling around me. Being on Tailcoat Jack's list was the last place I wanted to be, and I could have done without being in Ivan MacAlistair's debt. All things considered; I'd be lucky to get out of this mess intact.

It weighed heavy on me. I hardly slept last daylight. I needed a distraction. I needed some joy.

I needed me family.

The night air was still hot like an oven. The scorch of the sun still hung in the sky. William had told me stories of vampires so deep into their dark spiral that even dusk was as painful as the direct rays of the sun. I never wanted to let meself get that way.

Twilight was the last fleeting moments I had left of life in the sun. And I would withstand the discomfort just to watch the light shine through me windows each night.

I reached the North End as the air began to cool. I'd slipped on a modest dress from me stash of plain clothes I used when I visited me family. They would never understand how I'd managed to leave the old neighborhood and afford such expensive dresses. The less they knew the better.

Most of the streets of the North End were still dirt, a mostly underdeveloped landfill claimed from the waters of the harbour. The city did little to bring the new neighborhoods into the modern day. Not that the North End was all that new, the landfills were decades old. But the North End was where the Irish settled, marginally tolerated and largely unwelcome.

I'd worn a simple outfit, a few layers of dress, a shawl, and a lace crochet over me head. I didn't want to look like I was from downtown. I wanted to look like I belonged.

I wanted to *feel* like I belonged.

It wasn't unusual to find people milling about the neighborhoods after dark. Housing was shared among many families and living quarters were tight. Kerosene was expensive, so we burned whatever we had and hung around by fires on street sides, swapping stories and mucking about.

I followed the firelight through dirt roads and side streets until I found it.

Me family's home.

They were crowded around a metal basin filled with wood and fire. The smell of cooked meats hit me nose. Bangers roasted on sticks over the open flame.

The Murphy family was there too, and the O'Bradys.

Me father stiffened when he saw me.

"Siobhan!" me mother exclaimed. She got up and came to me, wrapping me in an embrace.

She took me face in her hands and smiled.

"I missed you, mum."

"Siobhan!" Mr. Murphy called out.

"Hey, lass. Good to see you," said Mr. O'Brady.

I got some waves from the teenage children between them. Me brother, Bradon, chucked his chin at me. "Where've you been dragged off to?"

"Living downtown. Still." I gave a sheepish smile.

"Well come, sit," mum said. "Get warm by the fire."

"Lot of laundry these days," me father said. It wasn't a question.

"Fergus!" me mother chastised.

Me father was unphased. He just stared me down.

I was a mix of emotions. There was fear. Every time I came here, I risked a great deal of trouble. William forbade me to see me family since me turning. Me dad's words stung. I was angry, but I was also hurt.

But looking into me father's eyes, behind that rough exterior, I could see he was hurt too. I'd walked away from me family to, as far as I told them, take a job downtown. I had given no warning. I just left.

"I get away when I can, but work sometimes takes me into the night," I said.

"How much laundry can they possibly have?" Bradon asked.

"I do more for them than laundry. That's why I live with them. I cook. I clean. Many things."

I hated lying to them.

"Not going to meet a husband toiling in some rich family's kitchen or basement," me father said.

"The money's good, Dad. In fact…" I reached for me purse. For tonight, I'd brought a simpler bag. It was bulky and made of cloth with a thick strap that went over me shoulder.

"Don't you dare come here handing out charity, girl," me father snapped.

I stayed me hand.

"I want to help," I explained.

"Keep it. Work on the docks has been steady. We're fine."

Me mum cast her eyes down. I frowned.

"Where are Moira and Fiona?" I tried changing the subject.

Me father didn't take the bait. Bradon answered instead. "They're off playing with some other neighborhood kids by the water."

"What happened to your eye?" I leaned towards Bradon.

"Eh." His tone was dismissive. "Three Know Nothings cornered me. You should see *them*, though."

"You were stupid. I told you not to walk home alone," me father scolded.

"What you need is a shillelagh!" Mrs. Murphy said. "Fergus, why haven't you got the boy a proper fightin' instrument?"

"Because we're not in the bloody factions and he shouldn't need one," me mum said.

"That shiner would beg to differ," Mr. O'Brady said. He pulled his stick from the fire. The sizzling sausage brought back a rush of memories. I missed the taste of food. Real food.

I watched Mr. O'Brady take a bite. Envy filled me eyes.

"No wood around here worth shit anyway," me dad said. He pretended not to notice the looks his wife was giving him. "We would need to leave the city out into the country. Maybe ash or oak. Brine it up good."

"Can we, dad? Me own shillelagh?" Bradon almost bounced at the idea.

"We'll see."

"You gotta teach him. Making it is only half the lesson." Mr. O'Brady stood up and held his now meatless stick aloft. He poked Mr. Murphy with it.

Little Jimmy Murphy let out a laugh. Mr. Murphy cuffed his son and then batted Mr. O'Brady's stick away.

"Come on, old man!" Mr. O'Brady got in a fencer's stance.

"Take him, dad!" Jimmy said.

"Fine. You want I should throw you a beatin'?" Mr. Murphy pulled his stick from the fire. He plucked the hot banger from its impalement and woofed it down. "Gimme a minute. Ow! Hot!"

"You'll burn your mouth off on that thing, you jackass," me father said. The adults laughed.

Soon, the friendly combatants were on their feet, pointing campfire sticks at each other.

"Avast!" Mr. O'Brady cried and lunged at Mr. Murphy. The tomfoolery got a laugh from the group of us.

Mr. Murphy parried, and the match was on. The two grown men swatting at each other like boys playing knights. Yet, for all childlike play, their fencing forms were own point. I noted the two men knew how to fight quite well.

Me dad stroked his chin. "Mind your right side, Mikey."

"Shut it, McQueeney," Mr. Murphy quipped. "No helping."

Sure as spit, Mr. Murphy whacked Mr. O'Brady on his right shoulder.

"Told you," me dad laughed.

"Shut it," Mr. Murphy repeated.

The match went on. Mr. O'Brady shifted into a new stance.

Me dad disapproved. "Foolish. You're gonna get stabbed, Mikey."

Mr. O'Brady was poised to lunge. Or was he?

"No. It's a feint," I said.

"You're daft, look at his shoulders," me dad insisted.

"Look at his feet." I pointed out.

Mr. O'Brady thrust his stick out. Mr. Murphy brought his own to guard his chest. In the last second, Mr. O'Brady swept out of the would-be lunge and whacked Mr. Murphy on his side.

"Ow! You sneaky bastard!" cried Mr. Murphy.

A few of us chuckled at poor Mr. Murphy's expense.

"Good eye," me dad said to me.

"Ta."

"You been keeping up with it? Your fencing?" he asked.

"Not so much," I confessed. "I haven't anything to practice with."

"Maybe we should be getting *you* your first shillelagh."

"Her? No, she's a girl! You were going to make one for me," Bradon whined.

Me dad pulled his own stick from the fire and appraised the skewered banger affixed to the end. "First of all, I'll not be making you a shillelagh. You'll be doin' that yourself. And secondly, girl or not, your sister could whoop your ass."

"Fergus!" me mum scolded.

Me dad shrugged. "Tis the truth."

Bradon sulked.

"Take heart, little brother. I've had more practice at it than you," I offered.

"Don't mind him," me dad said. "He needs to learn that things in life are earned and not given."

With that, me father thrust his campfire stick towards me. The banger dangled from the end. "Go on, it's yours."

"No, I couldn't." A tinge of panic seized me.

"I insist. I know I can be rough sometimes. I just miss you is all. We all do. But it's damn good to see you, lass, and I want you to feel welcome."

Me mother looked at me with eyes that pleaded for me to take the damn offering. The sausage represented more than food after all.

I couldn't refuse it.

"Thank you," I plucked the treat from its stick. Me stomach tightened.

The savory scent of the banger filled the air with a delicious aroma. I truly did miss the taste of real food, but the consequences for eating were dire.

I was *able* to eat, of course. But after that? Me body rejected anything in me stomach that wasn't blood. Rejected in horrid, painful upheavals and retching as it expelled anything foreign from its confines.

I stared at the sausage. I was going to be in for a rough night.

But worse than that, once I ate it, I had a precious matter of hours before the sickness set in. Which meant I either had to cut me visit short or risk me family seeing me throw up what I'd eaten with a fair amount of blood along with it.

I was damned either way.

Episode Eight

Sickness

IT WAS DELICIOUS.

How long had it been since I'd eaten real food? More than two years, for certain. The sausage was sweet with a smoky tinge.

In less than two hours, I'd be throwing it up in painful upheavals, but for now? I enjoyed every savory bite.

Misters Murphy and O'Brady had returned to their seats around the fire, relinquishing their cooking sticks to the flames.

Time whiled away as conversations turned nostalgic. The men complained about work and spun tales of the old country. Mr. O'Brady was somehow thrown into a rant where he cussed out the Queen for what felt like twenty minutes. We laughed and enjoyed good times with family and friends.

Reality slipped away. I was home. Me life felt normal.

There were no vampires, no fae, and no curse gnawing at me to sink into its dark spiral. There was only joy and camaraderie. And I wanted it to last forever.

But all good things must come to an end.

Nausea crept into me stomach. The sickly pull on me gut told me I didn't have much time until me indulgence of fireside meats made a second appearance.

"I should go," I said. "It's getting late, and I have to wake up early tomorrow."

"You just got here," mum said.

"You can stay a little while longer. You haven't even seen your sisters yet," dad said.

Moira and Fiona were still playing with the other children down by the water. "I really must away, truth be told I'd slipped out in the night. It'd be best for me to return sooner rather than later."

That part was true.

Me father frowned. "Which is it? You need to sneak back to your employer's house, or you have an early morning?"

"Both." I stood up. "I'm sorry."

"Siobhan...," me mum pleaded.

"I'll come back in a few days, I just need to go." Me stomach churned in warning.

"Siobhan, sit back down. Don't turn your back on your family. We won't see you again for weeks," dad said.

"Fergus!" Mum scolded.

"Turn me back?" I bristled. "Do you know how much trouble I'd get in for coming here? Do you know how much I miss all of you? Don't throw that in me—" I clutched me stomach.

Oh no.

"I need to go." I picked up the hem of me skirt and ran off.

"Siobhan!" mum chased after me.

"Mum, I'll come back later! I promise." I couldn't shake the woman. She chased after me through the street.

"Siobhan McQueeney, you come back here and give a proper goodbye!"

I tried to keep running, but I doubled over. I braced me hands on me knees. I tried to hold it back. Me cursed body had no way to handle real food, and it was doing its best to eject it out of me.

"Siobhan? Are you alright?" Me mum approached me.

"Stay away!"

I couldn't hold it back anymore. In a painful heave, out came the contents of my dalliance. Whole bites unaffected by me dead stomach, soaked in blood to boot.

"Jesus, Mary, and Joseph! Siobhan!" Me mum rushed to me side and put an arm around me.

"Mum, I'm sick. You need to stay back or... you'll catch it."

Mum took a few steps back.

"I didn't think I had it." I gritted my teeth, trying not to retch again. "When I started feeling sick, I fled. I didn't want to alarm you, and I didn't want you to catch it."

"You threw up blood," her voice was a whisper.

"It's fine," I lied. "It clears up in a few—"

Another heave. Another painful expulsion of the unagreeable bits of me stomach. More blood.

I coughed. "Days."

"Siobhan—"

"Please, mum. Make me apologies. When I feel better, I'll come back. I promise." I mustered the strength to stand upright and give me mum a wan smile.

"You look like death," she remarked.

"I'll be fine. Just need to rest. Tell dad, alright? He's upset."

Me mum could only nod. She moved to hug me, and I held up a hand. "No, I don't want you to catch it."

She looked fit to cry and held a hand over her mouth.

"I'm okay," I lied again. Then I shuffled off into the night, ignoring the palpable stare me mum gave behind me back.

Me throat burned and the taste of bile hung in me mouth.

It was stupid of me to eat, but I couldn't have refused me father. Things had been so tense between us since I'd left, and I'd finally gotten a moment where things felt normal again.

I wandered through the North End, lost in me thoughts.

I should have been paying more attention to me surroundings.

"Guid evenin', Siobhan McQueeney," the Scottish brogue pulled me out of me introspection.

Tailcoat Jack stood in the dirty street before me. His fancy cane dug into the thoroughfare as he pretended to need it to support his weight.

"What do you want? I'm hunting." I lied.

"Ah doubt that, me little potato maiden. Word around the bleed is ye like tae bash gangs of Know Nothings who abuse the Irish. If anything, you're these peoples' champion, nae their hunter." His lips curled in a sickly smile.

"I was just leaving. Me hunting is elsewhere."

"You're nae a very guid liar, Siobhan McQueeney."

I frowned. Me stomach still felt like hell, and the last thing I needed to do was throw up in front of a fae enforcer. "I haven't done anything wrong."

"Well, you see, that's what Ah'm tryin' to find out. Did you ken Ah cannae find Fiddlehead? Odd that he cannae be found right after ye go around Crocus asking for him. Then ye come tae the North End tae… nae hunt. Ah wonder what you're up tae, Siobhan McQueeney."

"I was… getting information from the locals. On where they were jumped by Know Nothings. So, I could avenge them," I lied.

Jack bobbed his head. "A likely reason. Possibly. Or maybe there's something else here that brings ye by?"

"No." Me stomach heaved. I tightened me jaw. "Like I said, I was just leaving. Please excuse me."

I moved to walk past him, and he grabbed me arm.

"We're nae done here, lass."

He was stronger than a *sidhe* ought to be. "Let me go."

He tightened his grip. He leaned in and whispered. "Ah dinnae ken what you're up to, Siobhan McQueeney, but Ah'll tell ye three times, Ah'm goin' tae find out. And when I do, your guilty blood will slake me thirst for the rest of your unnatural life."

"Siobhan," William's commanding voice pierced through the darkness. And me fear.

Me creator walked up. His eyes fell to me simple dress. Then to Jack's hand around me arm.

Jack released me and turned to him. "William Donovan, such a timely appearance."

"Nothing so coincidental, I assure you." He put on a smile. "I followed you here. I noticed you looking around while I was doing a bit of business on the east side. I want to thank you for finding Siobhan."

Jack wrinkled his nose at William. He frowned. "'Tis nae trouble. But Ah'm wondering what happened to Fiddlehead. Have ye seen him?"

"No. Fiddlehead had to return to Otherworld. Clan business. He didn't say. I need a new driver if you have any recommendations."

Jack snarled and stepped up to me creator. "If Ah find out you've been lyin' tae me, the *Scáilic Predominance*—"

William stiffened. "I am still an elder of this bleed, Jack, and you will treat me as such. Let us both remember that you walk in two worlds. Don Esteban may turn the other cheek, but I doubt the *Scáilic Predominance* would be so lenient."

"An empty threat. What are ye goin' tae do, travel to Otherworld and appeal your case tae the fae lords?"

The conversation was going over me head fast. *Two worlds*? And was William really threatening *Tailcoat Jack*?

"Siobhan, we're leaving. Jack, good evening."

It was William's turn to grab me arm now, though not painful, he wasted no time in ushering me past Jack and down the street.

"Thank you."

"Save it. You've crossed a line here, Siobhan. You're lucky I came by."

We've had this argument dozens of times. "I'm only going to see them a few more times, then come up with a story of moving out of town. I'll send letters from then on, but that's it."

William shook his head. "It never works. What you're doing is dangerous."

"I can't just break it off with them completely. They're me family!"

"I'll not have this discussion with you again. You'll slip up. You'll make a mistake. You'll reveal us."

"I won't." I was getting desperate. I couldn't just sever ties with me family so suddenly.

"I am not asking!" he rounded on me, eyes baleful.

I cowered. In that brief moment, he had the look of the devil in his eyes.

He looked away.

"We need to get you focused. Your debt to Ivan must be repaid. You need to steal the Wheelock sword, and you and I need to form a plan."

Me stomach was having none of it. Between what I ate, the threat of Tailcoat Jack, and the prospect of me losing me family, the stress compounded with nausea.

I bent over and expelled the last of it, barely missing William's boots.

A scant few seconds passed between us in silence. I couldn't meet his gaze. I closed me eyes waiting for the yelling to start.

William put a hand on me shoulder. "Are you alright?"

I looked at him. The angry frustration in his eyes had been replaced with concern.

All I could do was nod. I wiped me mouth with the back of me hand.

"You ate food?" He already knew the answer to the question.

"Yes," I said, meekly.

"Did you throw up in front of them?"

I shook me head. "No," I lied. "We had a fire and some bangers. I ate one to keep up appearances but excused meself when I felt ill."

"People don't throw up blood lightly. Much less walk away after doing so. You understand the risk here? Tell me you understand."

I bobbed me head vigorously. "I understand."

"Good. Now let's get you fed. You must be hungry."

William stood by as I fed from a lone dock worker down by the wharfs. He was probably trying to get a head start on the next morning's work.

William had to charm him for me. I was still getting the hang of that trick.

"That's enough. You don't want to leave them weak or have them pass out. People ask questions," William said.

I withdrew me fangs and licked me lips.

"He's still quite open to suggestion. Give him something to remember when he comes around. Like I taught you."

I looked at the dockhand. "The bites on your neck will be gone by morning. They're just mosquito bites. You're done at work here tonight. Go home get some sleep."

The worker lolled his head to me in a lazy acknowledgement. "You have pretty eyes," he said.

"Thank you."

I moved from him and let William escort me away.

"Why did you tell him to go home? He could have kept working," William said.

"I thought you said sometimes people get drowsy after losing blood. I didn't want him to fall into the water if he passed out."

William laughed. "Only you would think of such things, Siobhan."

I didn't see what was so funny about it.

We made our way back to William's building. I was still feeling humbled by me earlier indiscretions. I wanted to fill the silence with conversation, but I didn't know what to say.

So, I thought of a neutral topic. "What did you mean by Tailcoat Jack living in two worlds?"

"I think you must already know the answer to that."

I'd suspected since meeting him. "He's a vampire. He's a vampire fae."

William gave a nod. "He is. And with his sudden interest in you, we need the Wheelock sword more than ever."

The Heist

"No, that won't work. And, to be honest, you need much more training for something like that," William said.

"But as a bat, I could slip into a small opening. A lot of these buildings have—"

"And then what? You'll be naked once you get inside. You'll be traipsing around Thomas' house in the nude. If he catches you, the shock of it will make it all the more difficult for you to charm him. And your *charming gaze* isn't exactly up to snuff."

I huffed. "Fine."

"Besides, once you got the sword, you can't very well turn into a bat and carry it out the same way you came in. You'll need to leave out the door. Naked."

"Alright, I get it. It was just an idea," I said. "So, what should I do?"

We spent more time planning. Most of me good ideas were shot down as victims of William's fussing. He was worried about tonight, and so was I. I'd never broken into someone's house and stolen anything. Hell, I'd never stolen anything in me life.

A mere two hours after me failed *bat infiltration* idea, I was standing outside Thomas Coffin Amory's front door.

It was eleven o'clock at night. We agreed I should go late enough where Mr. Amory would be asleep, but early enough to give me time to search his house, find the sword, and get home before the sun came up.

I wanted to go at midnight. William insisted on eleven. He was worried I wouldn't have enough time to beat the sun.

I wasn't sure if I should be touched that William worried about me escaping the harmful rays of daylight or annoyed that he thought I couldn't find a sword in five hours.

I pulled meself from me musings, and appraised the door to Mr. Amory's home.

A *deadbolt break*, William called it. It was the idea that our superior strength could cleanly pop a door's deadbolt or chain from its mooring within a doorframe and smash open a locked door with little mess and noise.

I lined up me shoulder with the door at the edge above the doorknob. *One good hit.*

I slammed the door with me shoulder.

"Ow!" pain lanced through me. The heavy door didn't budge.

I tried again. I pulled back and lined up me shot. William said I had to hit right where the edge of the door met the frame.

I collided with the door a second time. It did not yield. "Ow! Dammit!" Me shoulder throbbed.

Stupid door. Was I not strong enough?

To my horror, it opened for me. Not of its own accord, but by the master of the house. I was standing face to face with Thomas Coffin Amory.

I placed him in his early fifties. He looked tired. His hair was unkempt. He was wearing a robe over his sleeping gown.

"It's eleven o'clock at night, young lady," he groused.

Me chest tightened. In me anxiety, me curse slithered into me mind, and I was compelled to do what came naturally. Me charming gaze.

I locked eyes with him. "I'm sorry it's so late. I've nowhere else to go. Me husband threw me out. He's...." Me mind concocted a story. "He's taken a new lover."

The man blinked and his expression sobered. "Why come here of all houses?"

"You're Mr. Amory. You serve the city. I thought you could help."

Did my charm work? I wasn't certain. Was I supposed to feel something?

"Come inside," he said.

I followed him indoors. He led me through his foyer and into his parlour. Me tension only got worse. How was I supposed to steal from him now?

"I can't put you up for the night, a young woman such as you are. You understand. But I can give you money for a hotel. In the morning, perhaps we can see what a barrister might do for you and your philandering husband."

"Thank you."

His sudden calm and hospitality was unnerving. Had I charmed him?

"Please, sit."

I did the bustle shuffle once more, backing up into a sofa before sitting down. Mr. Amory took a seat in an armchair opposite from me.

As he held me in his gaze, I realized he was trying to puzzle me out. In that moment, it was all too clear that I had not charmed him.

I really needed to practice that.

"What's your name?" he asked.

I wasn't about to give him me real name. "Lisa. Lisa Cooper."

"Cooper? I didn't know there were Irish with that name."

"Me husband is English," I lied. Me father would probably disown me if I ever married an Englishman.

"That must be an interesting story, how the two of you got together."

"Yea." I gave a tight-lipped smile.

Mr. Amory's house was furnished in the typical style of wealth I'd seen in Nigel's and William's homes. But for Mr. Amory, there was a keen number of antiques on display. An old black powder rifle hung on the wall. Dishes and cups of pewter adorned the mantelpiece over his fireplace.

Above the mantelpiece was a portrait of a man in an eighteenth-century military uniform.

"That's Major-General John Sullivan. Revolutionary War hero. Painted by none other than John Singleton Copley."

Neither of those names meant anything to me, but I smiled to me host. "It's fantastic."

"Yes, one of the proudest pieces of my collection. I wrote a biography of Mr. Sullivan some years ago, his life and accomplishments."

"That's great." The awkwardness was tangible. I could have stabbed it with a fork.

Mr. Amory leaned forward. "Why don't you tell me why you're really here, Mrs. Cooper."

I'm not good at confrontations. I ought to be, considering what I've become, but I'm not. Mr. Amory's eyes pierced through me. It was nothing preternatural, but I hadn't the will to keep up my façade against his suspicious gaze.

"I'm... looking for something. An antique sword."

"I have many. Mostly Revolutionary War sabers. A few bayonets too." He leaned back in his chair. "Were you planning to bust my door down and steal one of them?"

Guilt compelled me to be honest with the man. I'd figure out a plan to steal from him later. I hated to have to knock him out.

"No, not particularly. I mean to say, I am after a very specific sword."

"Oh? And what is this sword?" He seemed amused.

"It's called the Wheelock Sword."

That confounded him. He stroked his chin. "Wheelock Sword," he repeated.

I could only nod.

"Well, I don't know about anything called *Wheelock Sword*, but I do have a sword made by Simeon Wheelock. Tell me, what do you know of this sword?"

I shrugged. "It's just a sword."

"Hardly. Who put you up to this? Who would send a young woman to burgle a house for a sword she knew nothing about?"

I looked into his eyes, conjuring the power of me curse again. I tried to ignite a spark between us, to capture and confound his mind. Mr. Amory seemed unaffected.

"Allow me to tell you, then. Simeon Wheelock was a blacksmith that lived out in Uxbridge about a hundred years ago. He made many weapons for the war effort. But among the most interesting things he made were blades of pure iron. These were swords mostly, a few bayonets. And one hatchet, I believe," Mr. Amory explained.

Pure iron? What the devil did Ivan want with a pure Iron sword? I think I knew the answer, and the thought of it terrified me. Just what sort of mad plot was I involved in?

Mr. Amory raised his brows at me expression as I attempted to puzzle things out. "Pure iron. Strange, isn't it? In his writings, he said he was convinced that the Continental Army would have need of such weapons. He said the British Red Coats had enlisted *faerie soldiers.*"

"That's mad," I tried to feign incredulousness.

Mr. Amory shrugged. "I have one of those swords in my collection. One of the last, I belief. The others were lost in time or melted down for other projects. It's a rusty old thing, crude and a little misshapen. Iron can't hold an edge well. But I purchased it at auction years ago as a peculiar piece of history."

I was at a loss for words. What now? Spring up out of me seat and knock him out? Force him to give me the sword? Buy it from him? Me mind wrestled between me next course of action and the dangerous implications of why Ivan needed the sword in the first place.

Mr. Amory rose from his chair. "Let me get it for you."

"What?"

"You seem like a desperate woman. I don't know why you need this old sword, and I do not think you're keen on telling me. Wait here, please."

He left the room. I was alone with me thoughts. What was going on? He'd just hand the sword over to me? Is this some kind of trick? Is he stepping outside to call for police?

Me mind raced. This was too easy.

I should leave. Come back with money. Buy it off him.

Despite me internal debates, I remained rooted to the sofa.

I don't know how long I waited. Ten. Fifteen minutes. It felt like an eternity until Mr. Amory walked back into the parlour.

The sword he carried barely looked like a sword at all. He held it reverently, one hand on the hilt and the other supporting the blade. The weapon was a dull brown color. The metal was coated in rust. It had a hilt, pommel, and crossguard which marked it as a sword, but the blade was crude, like a child's drawing come to life.

"I'm afraid time has not been kind to this old weapon," his tone was apologetic.

"I don't understand," I said.

"What don't you understand?"

"You said *let me get it for you*. Are you giving it to me?"

"Well, yes." He sat down, resting the blade across his lap.

"Why?" I was dumbfounded.

"There are a few ways this story could have ended for us, Mrs. Cooper. I elected to choose a teachable moment."

I shook me head a little, not following.

"You wanted this sword so badly that you attempted to break into my home, unarmed and desperate. If I had sent you on your way, you may have returned with... I don't know, perhaps some hooligans. Perhaps someone would have gotten hurt. Perhaps I would get hurt. Or worse."

He was right. I looked away, lest he saw the truth in me eyes.

"So here is my lesson to you. Be careful whom you entangle yourself with. What kind of person or people send a woman out alone in the streets at this hour to rob a man's house?"

He didn't understand. I do just fine alone late at night. I gave him a small smile.

"But more than that. Your first impulse was to knock my door in instead of coming by at a reasonable hour and just asking me. Perhaps I could have sold it to you or, simply given it to you if your reason was compelling."

"But you know neither my reason nor asked me to buy it."

"True, but therein lies the lesson. You assumed you had no other option because of your lack of faith in your fellow man. So, I choose to simply give it to you to restore that faith. And to let it be a gesture for you not discount the good will of humanity."

He held the sword out to me.

I took it. The metal was cold, and the rust stained me hands.

"Don't lose faith in kindness, Mrs. Cooper. In a civilized society, it's all we have left."

Something about those words resonated with me down to me very core.

"I won't," I promised.

Episode Ten

The Consequences of Iron

ME MIND WAS A cocktail of mixed and conflicting feelings.

I was coming down from the rush of getting caught breaking into a man's home, and I was reeling over the strange turn of events that led to the man giving me the Wheelock Sword.

The metal hilt felt cool in me hand. The hilt's leather bindings had long since disintegrated. The sword looked like a piece of shite, rusted and dull with a blade pocked with time and erosion.

Yet this sword was iron, and that supplied the last ingredient of me emotional tapestry.

Panic.

Ivan MacAlistair had charged me with obtaining a sword of pure iron. What was he planning? Was William involved? Was I involved?

I'd been told to deliver it directly to Ivan. William didn't want it in his house. Now I understood why.

A vampire caught with iron in their home could be in a lot of trouble.

What was Ivan thinking?

I made a plan to hand the sword over to Ivan and tell him I wanted nothing to do with whatever scheme he was concocting.

Satisfied with the plan, I renewed me resolve. I obtained the sword, I'd settle things with Ivan, and things would go back to normal. I just had to look on the bright side. Tonight was a victory.

"Hello, lass."

Tailcoat Jack's salutation slithered from the shadows. The vampire-fae leaned against a lamppost like a vagrant. The white of his teeth pierced the darkness and illuminated his devious grin.

Jack pushed himself off his post and strode towards me. Me heart raced.

I was alone on a deserted street.

"William is expecting me. I'm on me way home," I said.

"Oh, Ah'm sure. You're a girl worth checking up on, Siobhan McQueeney. Ye go asking 'round the Crocus Tavern about Fiddlehead, and lo and behold, no one's seen him in as many nights."

He stopped and leaned against his fancy cane. "Then you go huntin' in the North End, yet... ye dinnae hunt your own people, do ye? Odd that. You've been lyin' tae me, Siobhan McQueeney. So, I reckon I should follow ye one more night tae see where ye—"

His eyes fell to the sword.

"I feel a shiver up my spine, lass." Jack scowled at me. "Is that... *iron*? Ye carryin' an iron blade?"

I thought of a lie on me toes. "It's just a rusty antique. I'm going to sell it for money."

"Who makes a sword of iron and why?" His eyes were baleful.

I shrugged. "I haven't the foggiest."

Jack's frown darkened. "Drop the sword, lass. Ah'll nae ask thrice for it."

I froze. If I didn't bring the sword back to Ivan what would that mean? Would I still owe him a debt for Nigel's death? Would he kill me? And more than that, would Jack just let me walk away if I dropped the sword?

In my indecision, me hand tightened around the hilt.

Jack put one hand on the ball of the cane's top and another hand on its shaft. It was an odd way to hold the cane, bent over as he was.

Me chest tightened when I realized.

It wasn't just a cane. He'd poised himself to draw something from the shaft by its wee knob of a handle.

There was no way I was going to drop a sword if he was about to draw one of his own.

"Wait, please. Stay your hand." I hoped to talk me way out of this. "Let me pass. Give me two hundred paces and I'll drop the sword."

"And, leave tonight unscathed? Unpunished? I dinnae think so. Drop the sword now, or Ah'll cut you to ribbons."

"Seems you're going to run me through either way. Let's solve this without bloodshed." Me heart was pounding.

"You're nae in a position to bargain, lass." Jack pulled on the knob of his cane. A metal hiss cut through the air as a blade slid from its wooden confines.

Yet Jack did not move towards me.

I considered that.

"No," I said.

"No!" Jack shouted. "Ah tell you three times now, drop the sword!"

"Yet you haven't taken a step towards me. You're hundreds of years old. Vampire and fae. And you haven't moved a step towards me." I raised me blade and pointed it at him. Me heart was pounding, but I was sure as hell me instincts were right about this. "You're afraid."

Tailcoat Jack gritted his teeth. His face screwed up in fury. He cast his wooden cane aside and brandished his blade at me. "You..." the words ground from his gnashed teeth. "You should nae poise yourself so confidently in this predicament, *páiste*."

His face burned with anger, but his eyes betrayed his fear. This observation lit a small spark of courage within me. "I'm the one with the iron sword. You're the fae."

I watched as his eyes darkened from fear to hatred.

Uh oh.

Tailcoat Jack charged me.

He was fast, but me father taught me well. I saw his lunge coming, and I parried. I withdrew a step to buy meself more time.

This was not how I wanted tonight to go.

Every strike, thrust, and slash from Jack was aimed at me throat. He was trying to decapitate me. I put me free hand up in front of me neck while I continued to parry as I retreated backwards.

There was a madness in his eyes. There was a burning fury and hatred that fueled his unrelenting attacks.

One of his swipes cut into me wrist where it guarded me neck. It would have been me throat had I not been blocking it.

The cut stung and I cried out. I swiveled and spun on me back foot. I tried not to give him a chance to follow through.

His next slash cut me in me shoulder. I cried out again.

I needed a new plan, or he'd whittle me down in no time.

Me father taught me how to fence. There were a couple of ways to fight with a shillelagh and fencing was one of them. I needed to pull meself together and let me training guide me.

I ducked down, bending at me waist. I thrust up from underneath and caught him with the point of me blade in his stomach.

It didn't go deep, but Jack let out a wailing cry of agony.

That small cut was more egregious than anything he'd landed on me. Jack backed off and cradled his gut.

"Let me go. Let me pass. And you and I will forget what happened here tonight," I said.

"There's no goin' back now, lass. Nae for either of us."

Jack held his wound and let his sword falter. I pointed me blade at him. "I've got you. It's over." As right as I was, me voice quavered.

I just wanted it to end. God, I just wanted to get away.

Jack shifted his weight. He raised his sword.

"Don't," I warned.

He moved on me. He tried to whack me sword away. A clank of metal rang out into the night as our blades met, but all I had to do was lunge.

Jack's sword slid fruitlessly down the shaft of me own weapon as me blade pierced into his chest.

His eyes went wide. He dropped his sword. It hit the cobblestone with a dull metallic ring.

I slowly pulled the blade from him. Mortified. "I didn't want this."

I'd never killed anyone before.

The color drained from Jack's face. He looked down at his wound and back to me. "I'm a cursed soul, Siobhan McQueeney. Do ye think they'll welcome me in *Tech Duinn*?"

He was speaking about Otherworld's Realm of the Dead, a sort of heaven for deceased fae as it were. Would one such as Jack pass through its proverbial gates? I didn't know how to answer that. I just watched in horror as Jack fell to the ground clutching his chest.

Instead of a firefly-like glimmer taking his body, he began to break down into ash and soot.

"Where will I go?" He asked me.

He looked terrified.

Tears streamed down me face as I watched his body, clothes and all, dissipate into smoke. His blackened remains blew away in the night air.

Then there was nothing.

"Unbelievable. Did anyone see you come to my door looking like this?" Ivan scowled at me. "Come inside."

I walked through his door. All I wanted to do was drop the sword and go home. I wanted the night to be over.

The image of Jack's body eroding into a cloud of ash still had me shaken to me core.

"What happened? You're all cut up, but you have the sword."

"I got the sword. I just want to go home."

Ivan frowned at me. "Did you have to kill Amory? It looks like you got in a fight. You need to tell me what happened."

"No, Amory's fine. He gave me the sword. He was kind."

"He just *gave* you the sword?"

I nodded.

"Then who cut you up like this?" Ivan's tone grew irritated.

"Jack. Tailcoat Jack."

Ivan threw his hands up. "Tailcoat Jack? Did he see you come here? How in the hell did Tailcoat Jack even—"

"He's dead."

Ivan's tirade came to a halt. His mouth hung open and he made an odd, dumbfounded sound. He furrowed his brows at me. "He's... dead?"

I raised the tip of the sword a wee bit. "Yes. I killed him. I'm sorry. But he attacked me and wouldn't let me pass."

"You killed him?" Ivan repeated.

He stared at me in silence a moment. Me heartbeat hastened. I just wanted to leave.

Then he laughed.

Peals of laughter erupted from the elder vampire. His grin was as wide as the horizon, and it revealed crow's feet in his eyes. Eyes that, for the first time, showed joy.

"You're sure? You're absolutely sure?" He clasped me shoulders and beamed at me.

"It was awful. He wouldn't let me pass. He was afraid of the sword, but too angry and prideful to let it go. I... stabbed him. Through the chest. And his body disintegrated into ash and smoke." I rubbed me eyes with the back of me hand.

"Brilliant! You wonderful girl!"

"What?"

"Who did you think this sword was for?" Ivan laughed again. "Oh, this is quite a turn of events. But we need to make haste. Run straight back to William and tell him what happened. We'll need to plan our next steps."

I held the Wheelock sword out to Ivan.

Ivan put up his hands. "Oh, no. I don't need that thing here in my house. The deed is done, and I've no further need for it. Take it to William. He may want to dispose of it, but I'll not have it here."

"But it's illegal to carry iron. I can't give it to William."

"Then throw it in the harbor. Might I remind you that you are still in my debt?" He shook his head, but then smiled at me. "I'm not angry. I'm very pleased. But let's dispose of that sword, yes?"

"Very well."

"Now go. Straight to William. Tell him the good news."

He all but pushed me out the door with a gleeful gleam in his eye. A moment later, I was standing on his front step, sword in hand.

I thought about throwing the sword in the harbour.

I looked down at the blade.

Throwing it away would be a mistake. There were still plenty of fae in Boston.

And William and Ivan were planning to overthrow them.

Maturity

"SIOBHAN IS THAT YOU?" William's voice greeted me when I walked through the door.

The building we shared had a central foyer and sitting room. Me plan was to dash upstairs and hide the Wheelock sword before finding William.

I held it in me hand, and if William walked into the foyer, he'd see me holding it.

Ivan thought it belonged at the bottom of the harbour, but I had other plans. Keeping an iron blade when things were this dangerous with the fae made good sense.

But I wasn't about to challenge me creator on that yet.

Next to me, a ceramic umbrella stand flanked the doorway. Two umbrella handles peaked out from their cylindrical confines. I slowly slid the sword between them.

I'd broach the subject about the sword with William later. After I'd told him I'd killed Tailcoat Jack.

William walked into the foyer looking worried. "You're back? You're alright?"

Before I could answer his eyes fell to me dress.

"You're cut. What happened?"

I told him everything. I spilled the entire story from Amory giving me the sword, to me fight with Tailcoat Jack, and to Ivan's elation. Halfway through me story, William had to stop me, so he could sit.

Panic settled into his face as I wove me story of Tailcoat Jack, but when I told him about Ivan's reaction, his expression grew thoughtful.

William stroked his chin and leaned back in his chair. "Interesting. Perhaps Ivan is right about this. But we must be cautious."

"What do we do now?"

"This accelerates our plans, but with Tailcoat Jack out of the way, we're in a good position. Siobhan, I want you with us. Ivan and I will need the support from here on out."

I grimaced. I didn't want to turn me back on me creator, but I really wasn't keen on plotting against the powers of the bleed either. "This is a lot, William. This is dangerous."

"I know. But you just removed a major cog of this oppressive machine. We have tentative support from a few others, but nothing we can confidently depend on. Ivan was going to bring in Nigel, but..."

"Right. Nigel." Me heart grew heavy at his name.

"You're the only one we can trust, Siobhan. We need you."

What was I supposed to say to that?

"Alright. I'm with you," I said at last.

"You misunderstand. I mean that literally. With us. By our side. Starting tomorrow night."

"Tomorrow night? At Don Esteban's soirée? I'm a *páiste*. No *páiste* are allowed at his parties."

William bobbed his head. "True. So, we accelerate some other things as well, namely your progression within the bleed. Tomorrow night, I will present you as having attained your *aibíocht*."

Me jaw fell open. *Me aibíocht?* The Irish word for maturity was a significant rite of passage and a message to everyone else in the bleed that I no longer needed the mentorship of me creator.

"But... I've still so much to learn. I need you."

"I will continue to mentor you and guide you in secret, but outwardly to the bleed, you'll be presented as mature."

"And I'll be responsible for me own actions, and you won't. Like me killing a fae noble."

"Siobhan." Me words had stung him. "How could you say that? You think I would let you fall for this? You think so little of me?"

"I... I'm sorry."

A heavy silence fell between us. William looked dejected. If I could have shrunk down to two centimeters and hid under the carpet, I would have.

"I'm scared. Tonight was horrifying. Watching Jack melt away into ash was ghastly. I feel like I'm in over me head. I feel like I'm drowning."

William got up from his chair and crossed the room to me. He put a hand on me shoulder. "I won't let you drown. You are as dear to me as if you were my own flesh and blood daughter."

I leaned into his chest and wrapped me arms around him. He returned the embrace, and I finally felt some sense of solace.

"Siobhan, I won't lie to you. It will become dangerous. I never wanted this for you. Not yet. The circumstances behind Nigel's demise thrust you into this plot. But that's why I want you with us. We are safer if we stick together. And that means starting with the soirée. And for that simple reason, and only that reason, I want to grant your *aibíocht.*"

"Truly?"

"You are a very accomplished vampire for one so young. I doubt you would have remained a *páiste* much longer. But don't worry, you will not soon lose me as your guide in this dark afterlife of ours."

All I could do was hold him tighter.

Jesus, Mary, and Joseph. The more wealth you have, the more layers of clothing you have to endure.

I loved the beautiful dresses of me new life, but getting ready was a chore unto itself.

Over me normal underclothes came a crinoline. The garment was a bell-shaped cage from the waist down. The crinoline bounced and swung about as I wrangled the other objects of me ensemble. Two petticoats followed, one over the other. Next, I tied pockets around me waist.

I kept a few personal effects in me pockets. I had some money, me fan, some hair pins, and various other helpful baubles.

Over the pockets and petticoats came me skirt. The skirt was blue with black trim and ruffles. Its black lacey frills nearly touched the floor. Last came the bodice of matching blue and black. Its hem draped over the top of me skirt and further aided to suck in me waist. For a formal affair like tonight, the neckline was low and me sleeves dangled precariously over the tops of me shoulders, nearly exposing them.

Me mum would think it racy, as if her daughter was dressing like a saloon girl. But I loved the fashion.

I sized meself up in me mirror, swishing meself this way and that.

Damn, I look good.

But better than me own appraisal was coming down the stairs to find William waiting for me. He beamed at me, and his eyes lit up and followed me every step.

"You found the dress, I see," he said.

"How could I miss it? The box was nearly as big as me bed."

"You look stunning." He took me hand when I reached the floor. "I'd bought that dress some months ago, for your *aibíocht*, but I never expected you would be wearing it so soon."

"You're sure about this?"

He squeezed me hand. "You're ready." He let me hand go and stepped back. "How do I look?"

William wore a top hat, jacket and tails, gloves, vest, and a frilly cravat. He was impeccable.

"You look quite...dapper." My pause was only for effect, and I grinned at him.

"Dapper? I was going for debonair."

"Aw, so close." I laughed.

"What is that?" William looked beyond me.

I turned around. William walked past me and to the umbrella stand.

"Ivan made me take it. He didn't want it." I grimaced a little.

"So, you thought you'd just stash it in plain sight in our house? What were you thinking?"

I crossed the room and stood between him and the sword. "Hear me out. If there are more fae out there, having an iron weapon could be a good idea."

"And getting caught with one is punishable by death." William frowned at me. "You need to get rid of it."

"Fine." I grabbed the sword by the hilt. "We can dump it in the harbour on the way to the party."

"No, we're running late as it is. Just put it back. We'll deal with it later."

I slid the sword back into the ceramic stand and released it. "I'm sorry."

"Ivan can be slippery. He got what he wanted and foisted his problem onto someone else. It's not your fault. Keeping the sword as a weapon was a fair idea, but it's too risky."

"You're not mad?" Relief washed over me.

William chuckled. "Hardly. I'm quite proud of you. Last night you defeated a great enemy of our kind and tonight is your *aibíocht*."

We had a new driver.

William stiffened as the goblin swept his hand to usher us into the carriage. The new driver was dressed much like Fidldehead used to dress. He wore buckle shoes, a bowler hat, and long coattails. The stocky little fae bent at the waist as he invited us into our own carriage.

Me creator stiffened. "Who are you?"

"Apologies, mister Donovan. Since the sudden... departure of your previous goblin, I was the quickest available resource Don Santiago could find. He wouldn't *dream* of having one of his elders remain bereft of a driver."

William looked over his shoulder a moment and then inclined his head to me. He looked at the goblin. "How thoughtful. I am honored that Don Esteban saw to my issue personally."

"Think nothing of it. My name is Fishmonger. If you need anything, call my name three times."

William mustered a cordial smile from the frown forming on his face. "Splendid."

We climbed into the carriage. It was no easy feat squeezing through the tiny opening with me crinoline making me hips the size of a boat. The wire frame did its best to squish down and spring back to size on the other side. Fishmonger closed the door behind us.

A moment later, the carriage lurched as he took the driver's seat.

William raised a finger to his lips and let a frown reclaim his expression.

Episode Twelve

The Party

"I don't understand."

William leaned forward and whispered. "I did not formally request a new driver. Though, at this point, it's no secret that Fiddlehead is no longer with us. What worries me is that Don Esteban personally found a replacement for him."

"That means he suspects something. He's letting you know."

William made a pained expression. "We need to be careful around Esteban. He won't make a scene tonight. There'll be too many mortals present. But we'll need to make our move soon."

Our move?

Me chest tightened at whatever that could entail. "What do you mean?"

He scowled. "You, Ivan, and I will meet later. We can't discuss it here or at the party."

Me stomach turned sour. Me heart raced in me chest. I tried to stay calm, but I wrestled with the notion that I could be staked and left out in the sun, to burn to death for me crimes of treason.

What had I gotten meself into?

"Who else is with us?" I asked.

William held a finger to his lips. His voice was hush. "Not here. I'll tell you everything when it's safe to talk."

There was a reddish-brown stain on me dress. I wiped it away with me hand.

Rust.

I'd forgotten about the sword. A moment ago, I held it in me gloved hand as I explained to William why I'd kept it.

I turned me hand over to see me glove covered in rusty grime.

"Siobhan, are you listening?"

I quickly placed me hands on me lap, palms down. "Yes. I'm just nervous is all."

William smiled and reached a hand towards me. I offered me left hand, with the clean glove. He took it and gave it a squeeze.

"I won't let anything happen to you. I promise. You trust me, yes?"

I inclined me head. "Yes."

His hand lingered. "You're so warm." He leaned forward and touched me cheek. "How are you still so warm?"

"I don't know," I lied.

William withdrew his hand and leaned back. "You're not drawing enough on your power. Siobhan, this is why you have such a hard time changing to your bat and wolf forms. This is why you still struggle with your charming gaze."

I called it drawing on me *curse*. It wasn't power. It felt wrong. It was a vileness I could feel as it seeped into me and wrapped around me heart. Drawing on me curse always left me feeling horrified, as if I was staring into a mirror and found me own corpse staring back at me.

"My dear, you have a reservoir of power at your disposal. I am not telling you to hurl yourself down the dark spiral. It's a delicate dance. It's a balance. But you have untapped power that will help you with your gifts."

"Can we not get into this topic, tonight?"

"Very well, but we will revisit it once our other business is settled."

As if me stomach wasn't already in knots.

I opted for a subject change. "Tell me about this party. What can I expect?"

I caught sight of Don Esteban's home as we turned the corner onto Commonwealth Avenue. The massive edifice rose above the brick buildings that flanked it on either side. It was like a castle in the middle of the city.

Large, sand-colored bricks tightly fitted together gave the building the appearance it was hewn from a single, enormous piece of stone. The mansion had turrets like a castle. It had balconies affixed to some of its second and third floor windows. There were four chimneys.

If someone had built battlements atop its roof, it would have looked like a medieval fortress. The ostentatiousness of it aside, it made for a rather sensible place for a vampire to live. I absently entertained the idea of asking William if we should get a castle of our own.

There wasn't much conversation as Fishmonger opened the carriage door and let us out. He remarked about taking the carriage to the livery until the party was over. William all but grunted at him. I made a point of thanking him properly.

I reckoned it made more sense to be kind to him, lest he surmised we suspected him of being a spy.

We entered Don Esteban's house through a door attached to a street-side patio. This sort of real estate in the heart of Boston was unheard of. For the size of the lot he had, Don Esteban could have easily built a brownstone apartment complex and rented it out to dozens of families.

I had to pick me jaw up off the floor when we went inside. I'd never seen anything so lavish in all me life.

Everything was gold, or at least painted that way. I couldn't tell. The furniture, the crown moulding, and mantelpiece by the fire, all shined in luminous precious metal.

A goblin came to check William's hat and coat. I had nothing for him to take, which seemed more like ceremony than necessity. The evenings were quite warm.

I leaned a bit towards me creator. "Is all this gold?"

He shook his head and whispered. "Gold foil, I presume. Everything is wrapped in it. Still quite expensive."

There were a few other guests milling around. I didn't recognize any of them. I strained me ears to pick up on their heartbeats. It was a skill I had yet to master. Mortals had a certain natural cadence to their beats, whereas vampires were a little off.

After a moment, I concluded we were in a room of mortals. William had told me the event was *catered*. That meant there were mortals here for the bleed to dine on in some of the private chambers in the house. Public, or *Live feeding*, wasn't allowed.

Richard Davenport swept through the greeting room and made his way to William and me. He was dressed in a tuxedo, minus the white gloves.

William had told me Don Esteban didn't like to wear gloves because he said it *made him look like a Freemason*. Whatever that was supposed to infer.

"William! And... Shevon? Such a surprise." Richard looked perplexed.

William gave Richard's hand a shake. "Siobhan has recently attained her *aibiocht*. This is her first party among the mature."

Richard put on a smile. "Excellent. Well, congratulations, Shevon. And welcome, welcome! Let me show you both inside."

The room we were led into was... I wasn't sure what I should have called it. *Function room* seemed appropriate. The vast room had an open floor space where a throng of guests clustered together. The tall ceiling was decorated in a fantastic mural depicting beautiful horned women, bare-chested men with the legs of deer, and miniature people with the wings of butterflies. At the center of the ceiling, an enormous chandelier hung over the room. Its dozens of tiny kerosene lamps flickered and illuminated the entire area.

"Beautiful, isn't it?" Richard grinned at me.

I smiled and felt a little embarrassed for staring at all the opulence like a child. "Yes, it's quite amazing."

"Don Esteban loves his mythology." Richard winked at me as he indicated the mural.

"I'm going to mingle a little. Siobhan, please flit about and introduce yourself around," William said.

A pang of anxiety lanced me. That didn't sound like our plan. "I thought you wanted to stick together. Announce me *aibíocht* and all that."

"Part of achieving your *aibíocht* is that you don't need me to make your introductions for you. This is your first outing. Go, mingle, and have fun." William bore a smile, but his eyes impressed on me to obey.

Richard looked between us and seemed a little lost. "Shevon, let me show you around. In the spirit of your *aibíocht*, I'll simply treat you as my colleague."

He held his arm out to me.

"Thank you, Richard," I said as I shot William a look. I looped me arm through Richard's and let him whisk me into the crowd.

"What was that all about?" asked Richard.

Despite me annoyance with me creator, I thought it prudent to cover for him. "Oh, he's just old fashioned. Now that I have me *aibíocht*, he wants me doing everything meself."

"Something to be proud of, to be sure. Especially for someone so young."

I cocked a look at him. His commentary sounded like a back-handed compliment.

"I should introduce you to Jacques. Have you met him?"

"No. But why are there so many people here?" There were far too many guests to dine on for the likes of our bleed.

"Not all of them are from Madam Poppy's *catering services*. Many of them are dignitaries, powerful socialites, and politicians. Remind me to introduce you to the governor. He should be around here somewhere."

The governor?

"But why the socialites? Are they here for us to—"

"Nothing so crass, I assure you," Richard cut me off. "Don Esteban is the richest man in New England. This party is a show of his influence and power."

Richard stopped and looked at me. "Power and control. As one who has come into her *aibíocht*, you should know that everything in the city runs by or through Don Esteban."

"Does he control them?" I whispered.

"No." Richard chuckled. "He doesn't need to. Believe me, for most men, money is a more potent elixir then all the charms in the world."

"But how does he…" I didn't finish me question. Madam Poppy sidled up to Richard and me.

"Richard! And your wee *páiste* friend." She frowned at us.

"Actually, Shevon just achieved her *aibíocht*," Richard beamed. He seemed to be enjoying prodding Poppy with the correction.

"So soon after her loss of control in me tavern? I find that rather concerning." Poppy's response was to Richard, but her eyes bored into mine.

Contrary to her dour demeanor, Poppy was a radiant vision in elegance. Her shoulders were bare like a saloon girl's. Her bright blue gown was impossibly form fitting with no discernible bodice. Attached to her modest bustle was a tiny train accented with white lace. Long white gloves ran past her elbows, and to top it off, a small tiara rested atop her head.

Beyond her glamour, her horns shined, polished to a fine luster. Her green eyes shone like stars in the sky.

For the mortals around us, their eyes continuously stole glances at her. Jealous women glared, and flustered men ogled.

"I apologize for the altercation, madam," I said. "But I've made great strides recently and me creator felt it was time."

"Well, this is fun," said Richard. "Poppy, I can assure you that—"

"Shut it, Richard," Poppy snapped.

Poppy looked me up and down and scowled.

This was not the sort of attention I wanted in Don Esteban's home. I shook me head at her. "I'm sorry for any trouble I caused."

Poppy seized me arm at the elbow. "Come with me, Siobhan McQueeney."

Richard protested, "Here now, I don't think this is the time nor place to air out your grievances."

Poppy ignored him and pulled me away and through the crowd.

"What's going on? Where are you taking me?" I asked.

"Someplace we can talk, *páiste*."

Dangerous Fraternization

Don Esteban's house was vast, but the party was contained within the giant hall on the first floor. Other areas of the house were restricted. Squat, surly goblins were posted in doorways to dissuade guests from wandering where they shouldn't be.

Madam Poppy pulled me towards one such doorway. Barricading the entrance was a stocky goblin in a green top hat.

"Beggin' yer pardon, Miss Poppy, but this way's off limits. If you want dining for yer um… friend, it's down the hall and to the right." The goblin tightened his lips. He seemed nervous.

As Madam Poppy took a step towards him, I could see why. He feared the *sidhe* woman.

"Step out of the way, Goatshove."

Goatshove? I could never get the hang of goblin names. Most of them came off like insults.

The goblin flustered. "Well, the thing is, this part of the house—"

"Now," Poppy demanded.

With that, Goatshove stepped aside. Poppy took me arm again and pulled me past him and into an adjacent room. The goblin resumed his post in the doorway behind us.

"What's going on?" I got the nerve to ask.

"What's your deal, Siobhan McQueeney?" She finally let go of me arm and leveled her gaze at me. Her bright green eyes bore into me.

"I don't understand. What are you talking about?"

"Dinnae play dumb with me, lass. I know all about the iron sword."

Me stomach rolled over upon itself and me heart nearly seized. "What?"

Poppy scowled at me. "The sword. Simeon Wheelock's iron sword."

"I don't know what you're talking about."

"You're lying. I can *smell* the iron on ye."

That couldn't be true. I frowned at the notion. How could she possibly...

I'd forgotten. Me hand was covered in rust and iron from having handled the sword earlier tonight. I absently placed me palms down against me dress.

"What are you going to do?" I didn't want to know her answer. I wanted to shout for William.

"What am I going tae do? What are *ye* going tae do?"

"What? Nothing? I don't even know what's going on." That was partially true.

She cocked her head at me. "Then why would Thomas give *ye* the sword?"

It was her emphasis on *you* or rather *ye*, that threw me off. Confusion replaced panic.

"Alright, Madam. Speak plainly. I barely know half of what's going on and that's the truth."

She huffed. "*Páiste*. William's a fool. Thomas gave ye the sword, aye?"

I nodded, despite me better judgement.

"We need that sword in the hands of one of our own, not some *páiste*."

"I'm not a *páiste*." I snapped.

"The hell you're not, lass. How did you even know about the sword?"

"Ivan told me. Alright, I answered your questions, now you answer mine." She had me annoyed, and that kindled me boldness.

Poppy arched her brows at me. I ignored her attempt to look affronted.

"What's a *sidhe* interested in an iron sword for?"

Me question hit her like a slap in the face. Her steely gaze broke, and her shouldered slumped. In spite of it all, I regretted being so curt with her.

"I hate it." She met me gaze at last. "I hate all of it. This filthy city. The darkness. The vampires. My own people becoming monsters like you."

I tried not to let that sting me, but it did.

Poppy shook her head. "Ye think I want tae run some despicable club where mortals are bled like cattle for you lot? I want tae go home! I want tae return tae the great mounds and sing and dance and play music. I am *sidhe*. I'm not some damned blood merchant."

"I'm so sorry. I didn't—"

"Save it," she snapped. "What are ye going tae do with the sword?"

Suddenly, the prospect of killing our fae overlords didn't sound like such an enticing mission. I tightened me lips before answering. "Drive you lot out, I imagine."

"I'll go willingly. But you need tae—"

A man approached us. He was silent and I'd been so wrapped up in me conversation with Poppy, I hadn't noticed until he was in me peripheral vision.

"Is this her?" the man asked.

I knew him. I'd never met him before, but William spoke of him often. Ian Hayworth was an elder in the New England bleed alongside William and Ivan.

Ian's dark skin was slightly paled by his curse. He was dressed in all the latest finery, replete with embroidered waistcoat, patterned vest, and fine boots. He was wealthy, which for a man of color in this country, even in abolitionist-friendly Massachusetts, was something of a sticking point to many people.

Good for him, I say.

But his sudden appearance and obvious involvement in all this plotting wreaked havoc on me nerves.

Poppy gave Ian a quick nod. "'Tis her. She's in over her head, says I."

"Does she have it?" he asked.

"Aye. But I think it would do better with you."

"Sorry," I interrupted. "Shouldn't William be part of this conversation?"

"No," Ian said. "We shouldn't be having this conversation at all." He took a moment to look around the room and give emphasis to his point. "At least not here."

He gave a slight bow. "Ian Hayworth."

In proper response, I inclined me head. "Siobhan McQueeney. I've reached me *aibíocht*."

Ian chuckled. "Have you now? Well, congratulations, Miss McQueeney."

I still didn't know whether or not I should be rolling in panic. I wasn't confident I was in good standing with Poppy and Ian. I fanned meself. "Is it hot in here?"

"No." Ian gave a smile. "But, we should rejoin the party. We don't want to attract attention."

"I needed to sort her out," said Poppy.

"And we will, just not here. I'll contact William and Ivan and see what's what," said Ian.

A chill ran up me spine. Richard and another man approached our little gathering. Though, I'd never met him in person, I recognized the man to be Don Esteban Santiago.

The lord of the New England bleed was shockingly handsome. I almost forgot to panic at the very sight of him. He had sharp cheekbones, a square jaw, and one of those dimples in his chin. His hair was dark and bore slight curls. Despite his curse, Don Esteban's brown skin was exotic. I'd never seen anyone from the Mediterranean region before.

Beyond his chiseled features, Don Esteban had a muscular build that forced his jacket's sleeves and breast to tighten to and fro as he moved.

Lost in me brief admiration, I'd missed a conversation unfolding around me. All at once, I realized all eyes were on me.

"Don Esteban. What an honor it is to meet you in person," I said.

The vampire lord looked amused.

It was Richard who responded, "Shevon, Don Esteban asked you how you were doing this evening. He's a little surprised to find you and some of his guests off in some room together."

Me heart sunk, and me stomach tightened. *How do I explain that?*

Don Esteban smiled like a cat to a mouse. "It's quite alright. The young lady looks a little flummoxed. But yes, my scion is correct, I am curious as to what this little gathering is all about."

Ian chimed in, "Young Siobhan here has attained her *aibíocht*. We needed to talk about dining arrangements away from mortal ears. Madam Poppy was just explaining where bleed guests go to feed."

Don Esteban held Ian in his gaze a moment. "Is *that* what this is?"

Ian stiffened. "Of course. She's never been to one of these parties before."

Poppy sucked in a breath. Richard put on a smile and aimed it at his creator.

The vampire lord swept his gaze back to me. Instead of a bow, he offered his hand. William told me he might try to shake me hand. It's a little old fashioned for a gentleman to do these days, but Don Esteban was quite old, and I wasn't about to correct him.

I shook his hand.

Don Esteban smiled at me. "Well, it is a pleasure to—Agh!"

He ripped his hand from me own. "Your hand. It's like fire!"

Richard, Ian, and Poppy looked shocked over the display. Panic seized me from toes to crown.

What had I done?

Don Esteban looked me up and down. He shook out his hand. "It was nothing. Nothing. A joke, yes? A young vampire with skin so warm." His face broke into a chuckle, but his eyes still harboured a malicious bite.

"Well," Ian began, "let us break up this little side group and rejoin the party, shall we?"

"Yes. Let's." Esteban's tone was curt, and his eyes never left me. "I trust there will be no more wandering around my home?"

I simply shook me head at him.

"Splendid. Come, Richard. Let's check on our other guests." With a flourish, Don Esteban spun on his heel and swept from the room. Richard followed on his coattails.

The rest of us moved to leave the room as well. I just wanted to go home. Everything was getting out of hand.

Poppy cut in front of me. "Take this." She thrust a gold coin at me.

I reached for it. Poppy pulled it back. "Other hand."

I took the coin with me left hand, the hand not soiled in iron.

I inspected the coin. It had a tree on one side and the face of a woman on the other. Irish writing was carved around its boarder.

"What is this?" I whispered.

"An invitation. Show that to the doorman at Crocus this Thursday night," she replied.

Ian had already hastened from the room. Poppy turned and followed, leaving me standing in the room holding a gold coin.

"But..." I was confused to beat hell.

Poppy turned back to look at me over her shoulder. "Check your right hand."

Then she disappeared into the crowd across the room.

I looked at me right hand. Iron still stained me glove. Iron and...

Ash.

Don Esteban said me hand felt like fire.

Episode Fourteen

Conspiring

I'd elicited me fair share of stares after retreating back into the press of people within the function room.

The *outrage* of it all, a woman unaccompanied, just flitting about the party like a floozie.

And this was supposed to be an advanced society compared to me muddy village back home? At least there, I could talk to whomever I damn well pleased whenever I wanted.

I shook off the reproachful looks and found a place to sit and wait for William. I was quite angry with him. He'd left me alone just long enough to be waylaid by both Poppy and Don Esteban.

The entire evening had me on edge. I surveyed the crowd. There were only a handful of vampires at the party. They milled in and out of the function room as they stepped out to feed. There were no fae, save for Poppy and the goblins. The rest were mortals.

I wanted to turn invisible. I wanted to leave. I didn't feel safe, and the longer I sat alone, the more irritated I became with William.

Where the hell was he?

It was another half hour before I spotted him again. He and Ivan sashayed into the function room with their eyes sweeping the crowd.

I dug me fan out of me dress pocket and unfolded it with a snap. I waved it at shoulder length to grab William's attention.

God forbid me, a woman, called out to him from across the room. Think of the horror.

It took a while for him to spot me, but he smiled and made a beeline towards me.

"Siobhan!" He looked this away and that. "All alone?"

"You left me without a chaperone." I scowled.

"You were with Richard when I left you."

"He's off with Don Esteban." I fluttered me fan in annoyance.

"Are you upset with me?" He looked dumbstruck.

"We need to go. I'll explain everything." I rose from me chair.

William shook his head. "It's much too early. It would be crass." He took a step towards me and whispered. "Whatever it is, it will have to wait. Let's just enjoy the party and we'll leave in a couple of hours."

Frustrated, I showed him the palm of me hand. The glove stained with rust and ash.

"What's this?" He took me hand. "Siobhan, your glove is filthy. Is this...?"

He looked at me. I widened me eyes to urge him to see the point I was making.

William looked back down at me hand. "So... did you meet Don Esteban?"

"I did. And Ian Hayworth. And Poppy and I talked for a bit."

Me creator's mouth dropped open. "Did I leave you alone for so long?"

"Long enough."

"Very well," he said in a hush. "You've made your point. But we still can't leave early. It'll rouse suspicion. Come. Let me introduce you some of the other guests. Don Esteban has invited many influential Bostonians, and one can always benefit from making acquaintances with mortals in positions of power."

He offered his arm to me, and after I scrunched me nose at him, I took it.

The remaining two hours moved at a snail's pace as I was introduced to a parade of sycophants, debutantes, socialites, and well-dressed philanderers. It was insufferable, but I put on me best smile and inclined me head to each of them.

William was a well-connected man. His own wealth and power had a little coterie of its own. Within a matter of minutes, we had an entourage of guests clinging to us and being ever so excited to meet me, his *business associate*.

They never even asked me what I did.

At last, the evening wound down and the party-goers offered thanks and well wishes to our host, Don Esteban. Me stomach tightened as we made our way up the procession for our turn to thank our *liege* and bid him farewell.

"Ah, William. Thank you for coming." Don Esteban clasped his hands over me creator's. "So nice to meet your young scion." He flashed that predatory smile again.

"It was a lovely evening, Don Esteban. We're looking forward to the next."

"I'm sure, I'm sure. And Miss McQueeney! Congratulations on your *aibíocht*. Such a magical time for a... well, one such as we."

He didn't take me hand. He bowed instead, and I inclined me head. "I was honored to be welcomed into your home, Don Esteban. It was lovely to meet you."

Don Esteban leaned in close. He locked eyes with me and whispered. "You'll forgive me if I don't shake hands. You're a bold one, I'll give you that."

He leaned back and smiled. His eyes never left mine. "Until we meet again, Miss McQueeney."

The pit of me stomach turned sour, and ice ran up me spine. All I could do was smile back.

Once outside, William turned to me. "What was that all about?"

"You heard that? What he said?"

"Of course I did. *You're a bold one*?" William frowned.

I showed him the palm of me glove again. "Iron and ash. Don Esteban is fae."

William smiled and suppressed a chuckle. "Siobhan, Esteban isn't fae. We see him as plain as anyone else. There is no glamour. He has no pointed ears or horns. You're mistaken."

"No. This ash was left behind after he shook me hand. I burned him. He yanked his hand away and said me hand felt like fire. I've got iron stains all over me glove. See?" I held me hand closer to him.

William gently eased me hand away. "There has to be some other explanation. Fae do not look human. And if he was using glamour to hide his appearance, we'd see it. It is among our gifts to penetrate the obfuscations of the fae."

"But the ash...," I persisted.

"I will speak to Ivan about it." William looked over his shoulder. Guests were spilling out into the street and milling around us. "We can't speak freely here. Let's go home and you can tell me everything."

We were driven home in short order. William and I kept quiet in the carriage, lest Fishmonger overheard anything. As me mum would say, we trusted him about as far as I could throw a cake underwater.

A tremendous weight lifted off me when we finally walked through our front door. We were home. We were safe.

I didn't waste any time returning to our pressing conversation. "So, you think Don Esteban knows? I burned him when I shook his hand. What do we do? He knows that I know he's fae." I found meself pacing.

"Siobhan, please. Take a moment."

"Do we even have a moment? Are they going to come and take us? Arrest us? How does this even—"

William put his hand up.

I folded me arms, a little irritated that he wasn't as panicked as I.

"The *Scáilic Predominance* has rules. No one is going to come arrest us or kick our door down. The bleed is bound to the laws of the fae who keep order. The irony of our dilemma is that the very people we are looking to overthrow are the ones mired in procedure. We have time, but not much."

William's demeanor was calm, and I found meself relaxing.

"How much time?" I asked.

"A few nights maybe. What did Poppy and Ian want with you? What did they say?"

"It was all such a blur. I think Poppy isn't like the others. She's working with Ian against the Predominance, I think. She's miserable here. She wants to return to her fae world, whatever that means."

"We call it Otherworld. Many fae feel as she does, but it's hard to tell whom to trust. Her dealings with Ian are known to Ivan and me, but we've been cautious about approaching them."

I fished the gold coin from me pocket. "Poppy gave me this. She said I should come to Crocus this coming Thursday."

William took the coin and inspected it. "An invitation? A secret meeting no doubt. Will Ian be there?"

"I don't know."

"You should go and see what you can find. Perhaps we can combine forces."

"Can we trust Ian?" I asked.

"Ian? I would think you would be more concerned with Poppy."

"I remember you telling me that Ian's scion is Henry Thatcher. I met Henry in Crocus some nights ago. You know he's a Know Nothing? Why would Ian turn someone like that?"

William looked thoughtful and took a moment before answering. "At first, I thought he did it as retribution. As the story went, Henry had some rather disparaging words for Ian based on the color of his skin."

I frowned. "That's a typical Know Nothing for you."

He gave a small shrug. "But it wasn't a punishment. Ian saw it as a challenge to take the young man under his wing and teach him to be better."

"That's an interesting reason to bestow the curse." I scoffed.

"It's not a—"

"I know, I know. I'm just saying that it's a little ironic that Ian thought it better to turn Henry into a vampire than let him remain the absolute *merkin* he was in life. What made Ian think it was a good idea to grant a man like that strength and power?"

William smirked a little. "Ian is a complicated man. You and he have a bit in common, actually. His disposition is rather optimistic for people like us, and he's done his best to maintain the moral compass he had in life."

I smiled at that. I liked knowing there were others like me, and an elder to boot. It was comforting knowing someone with a similar philosophy had staved off the dark spiral for many years.

"Don't become too enamored with Ian. His reluctance to embrace his power has left him weaker than most vampires his age. It's dangerous to be so old and so overmatched by your peers."

I gave a conciliatory nod, but I was still very interested in the secret to Ian's success.

"Now then," William began, "we are going to have to keep our noses clean these next few nights while we plan our next move. I want you to go to Crocus on Thursday, but that's it. Do you understand? No more trips to the North End. It's time you cut your ties."

The subject of abandoning me family always made me stomach uneasy. Anxiety seized me heart. I knew I'd have to do it eventually, but I was never ready. I certainly wasn't ready now.

"I understand," I placated.

"I mean it, Siobhan. It's dangerous. For you. And for them. You don't want them mixed up with Don Esteban, do you?"

"No! Of course not." Me heart tightened even more.

William held me in his gaze a moment before he was satisfied. "Good. Now go and get changed. I don't know about you, but I didn't find time to feed at the party. Let's go hunting."

"Yes, William."

I broke off and made me way up the stairs. An anvil lay in the pit of me stomach. I couldn't bear the thought of never seeing me family again.

I knew the day would have to come, before so many years had passed, and they wondered why I hadn't aged. But I wasn't ready.

Perhaps I could explain things. Tell them I was moving away. Then they would know why I lost contact with them. They'd have an explanation, and they wouldn't fear the worst.

Me mind reeled with a myriad of ideas as various scenarios played out in me head. No matter what I had to tell me family, I had tell them something.

One more trip to see me family. If I was careful, William would never know.

Tomorrow night.

Episode Fifteen

Lucy

I'M SOMEONE WHO FINDS great joy in small victories.

The last three years of me life as a vampire had not been easy. I'm not talking about the obvious horror of being a vampire, rather the supposed *gifts* that we are supposed to possess.

I have trouble shapeshifting to me bat and wolf forms. I'm only marginally faster and stronger than I was in life. And me charming gaze has not been the hunting tool I've needed it to be.

Until last night.

William and I had gone hunting, and he let me take the lead. I don't know if it was me adrenaline after an evening at Don Santiago's or the simple fact that I was so damn hungry, but I did it. I charmed me quarry.

William was quite proud, of course, and that gave me all the fuel I needed to manipulate me creator to get what I wanted tonight.

I knocked on William's chamber door.

He answered in a state of mid-dress. He wore trousers and a shirt but no other trappings. It was still early.

"You're already dressed? Still getting up at dusk?" he asked.

"Twilight doesn't affect me the way it does you. Not yet, at least."

"Give me a moment. Did you want to hunt again? You did well last night."

"About that, I was thinking of hunting alone tonight," I said.

"Oh?"

I bobbed me head. "Me charming gaze went off without a hitch. I think I'm getting the hang of it, but I think it would be easier to charm someone if you weren't at me side."

"That's true. I sometimes worry that my presence is distracting to our quarry."

"So, may I? Go hunting alone?"

William ran a hand through his hair. He searched me eyes a moment. "Part of us hunting together is for safety. I worry that Esteban is on the move."

"If you thought he'd be striking tonight, we'd be meeting with Ivan. Please? I need this. I need to know that I can do it."

"You *have* done it. Last night and before. You just haven't been consistent."

"All the more reason for me to get more practice." I smiled at him.

William let out a breath. "Alright fine. But stay close to the neighborhood, and be back soon."

That would throw a kink in me plans, but at least it would get me out the door alone. I gave William a quick nod. "Of course."

He smiled at me and put a hand on me shoulder. "I'm proud of you. Now go and come back, so that you and I can do something more meaningful tonight. I thought we could take in a play."

Guilt settled into me. I had no intention of returning early. I was off to see me family.

One last time.

The streets of Boston were still quite busy an hour or so after dusk. It's often why I chose to hunt later in the evening, but tonight I wasn't hunting.

The bustling streets made me anxious. After spending an evening with the city's elite, I didn't want to chance being recognized.

I took side streets and alleys as I made me way to me old neighbourhood.

I paid close attention to me surrounds as I went, making sure no one was paying any more attention to me than they should. If even one person recognized me, that information could get back to anyone in the bleed. I wasn't supposed to be going to the North End. If anyone saw me, I'd be in a lot of trouble.

I liked it better when I was a nobody.

Dread washed over me when I realized me paranoia was justified. I was being followed.

She followed me down Congress Street. She tailed me through the Faneuil Hall marketplace. I couldn't shake her, and the streets were still a bit too crowded to confront her.

I stole a glance at her over me shoulder as I quickened me pace. From one hundred meters or so, I couldn't make out much. She dressed well, she appeared to be a young woman, and she had the unnatural speed and stamina enough to keep up with the likes of me.

Yet, as I narrowed me eyes and tried to pierce her glamour, I could find none. She wasn't fae, but no mortal could keep pace with me for this long.

Then again, I remembered Don Esteban. He had no glamour either and yet, iron burned him. Was this woman something like Esteban? What was she?

I picked up me pace, but I was getting close to the North End. Whatever she was, I didn't want to lead her back to me family.

I found an alleyway adjacent to Cross street. The derelict street was vacant. It was perfect.

Sure enough, me stalker turned down the same path and followed me down its dirty cobblestones.

I stopped and turned to face her. The woman was still some distance away, but she stopped as well.

"What do you want? Who are you?" I asked.

Me vision is quite keen at night, but with the distance between us, I still couldn't make out her features. Her dark hair was done up under a fancy hat, but her face was tilted downwards. I couldn't see her eyes.

"Siobhan, wasn't it?" she replied.

"Who are you?" I repeated, a bit more forcefully.

She lifted her chin and smiled at me. She was stunning. Her brown eyes were like pools that I was sure many a man drowned in. Her skin was almost earthy, not unlike Don Esteban's but not quite the same either. She had high cheekbones and a round face. She reminded me of something chiseled from marble brought to life. Like Aphrodite or Athena.

She walked towards me. "You don't recognize me?"

It took me a moment. It was her. The woman who was bound in the chair all those nights ago. Nigel's prisoner, the woman with the powerful blood. The woman whose voice could bring a man to his knees.

"Leucosia?"

She gave a slow nod and stopped around twenty meters from me. "Call me Lucy."

"What are you doing here? What do you want?" I looked over me shoulder as a sinking feeling settled into me gut.

She held up her hands. "Nothing of harm to you, I promise. I came to find you."

"Why? And how *did* you find me?"

"I told you when you rescued me that we were bound. When the fates have need, our paths will cross. And tonight, the fates have led me to you."

"What are you talking about?"

"I had a vision." Lucy moved towards me again. Her gait was slow and cautious.

I scrunched me nose. Everything she had said so far sounded like nonsense. "A vision?"

"I have them from time to time. Glimpses of the future. Pertinent things for those close to me or dire things that affect us all. This vision was one from the former."

"So, you and I are close?" I didn't mean for my tone to come off so flippant.

"As the fates see it? Yes." She stopped within arms reach of me. Her posture was stiff. I knew fear when I saw it.

"I'm not going to hurt you, either."

She relaxed a little. "Good. I wasn't sure. I usually steer clear of your kind, but you're different."

"Different how?"

"Different from Nigel, at least. Would others of your kind have released me?"

I knew the answer to that. I made a face.

Lucy smiled. It was disarming, and I found meself relaxing too. "Precisely. Different."

"Alright. So, tell me about this vision."

"You're in danger," she said.

That, I knew. I slowly bobbed me head up and down. "Do you have specifics?"

"I saw you being attacked by horned men. *Sidhe*. I couldn't see how the entire fight will go, but I could see you were outnumbered."

Delightful.

"When?" I asked.

"I don't know. Soon, though. The events I see always unfold soon after I see them."

"Can it be changed? Is there a way to stop it from happening?"

Lucy shook her head. "No. The visions never lie. They always come to pass."

I furrowed me brows. I debated not going to see me family. I debated returning to William to tell him about this.

"I'm sorry," Lucy said.

"No, thank you for telling me."

"If I can find you when it happens, I'll aid you. The fae cause enough problems around here as it is."

That renewed me curiosity, despite the impending doom hanging over me head. "You're not fae?"

"Me?" She gave a laugh, a melodious little symphony unto itself. "No, I'm no fae."

"If you don't mind me asking... that is, I don't mean to sound rude, but—"

"A seiren."

"What?" I blinked.

"I'm a seiren." She offered an amused smile. "I figure it's safe to tell you, since you're a preternatural being yourself."

"I suppose I am." I had to wrap me head around what she'd just told me. "So, when you say seiren, you mean like the old stories of singing and sailors crashing into rocks?"

She laughed her singsong laugh again. "Well, yes."

I vividly remembered her shout hurling Nigel across the room. "That explains a lot."

"Just be careful. I like you, Siobhan. I don't have a lot of friends on the immortal side of the fence. Most things like us are out to kill me."

I had more questions, but the weight of Lucy's vision settled back onto me head again.

Lucy looked over her shoulder. "I should go. I've known about Don Esteban for a while, but now he knows about me. And this is much closer to his territory than I care to be."

"I didn't tell—"

"I know you didn't. My guess is that you had to explain what happened to your friend, and word got around. I don't blame you. But, yes, I'm being hunted." She smirked as if she'd just made a joke.

"Well, stay safe." I offered a wan smile. "And thank you."

"Stay safe, yourself." she offered her hand.

Ladies didn't shake hands. I couldn't help but grin at the gesture. She must have been like me, born of a different culture, unbound by the trappings of so-called civilized society.

I shook her hand, and her eyes filled with amusement.

"What?" I asked.

"Your hand is warm. You're an odd vampire, you know that?"

"Thank you." I chuckled.

We parted, and she made her way out. "We'll meet again, Siobhan."

I didn't doubt it. I watched her disappear down the alley.

Lucy's vision galvanized me desire to see me family. I resumed me trek towards the North End. This damnable plot that I'd been dragged into was going to change me life forever. Maybe I wouldn't survive it. Maybe I would be thrust into some new, deadlier arena.

This bleak life of mine was only going to get darker and more dangerous. And in that hardship, I only had a finite number of people who truly cared about me.

And I wasn't about to push any of them away.

Episode Sixteen

Return To The North End

THE NORTH END WAS Boston's forgotten stepchild. About twenty years ago, the streets were booming with new construction and opportunity.

Then the Irish came. We weren't welcome, and the Yankees had no desire to be our neighbors. They moved out. Retreating property owners divested their interests to slum lords who did nothing to improve land no one wanted.

The nicer parts of the North End had been built before the immigrations. Yet even the fine townhouses were converted into cheap tenements, crammed with multiple families in each apartment.

Me family was not in a position to rent within one of the brick buildings. They'd settled into a wooden house in a neighborhood where most of the streets had yet to be cobbled.

Despite the run-down landscape and neglected architecture, a wave of serenity washed over me as I plodded me way down me family's street.

I was home, and all the dirt and disrepair of the North End couldn't sour me mood.

Me family's home was a tall, thin building. Its width was little more than two windows wide. The exterior dilapidated clap boards marked it as newer and cheaper than its brick neighbours.

The three-story apartment was shared between me family, the Murphys, and the O'Bradys. Living quarters were cramped. They shared a kitchen. There was one bathroom. But it was the best they could all afford.

I knocked on the door. It took a moment for it to be answered. Me father's eyes were weary, and it took him a few seconds to register who I was.

"Siobhan?"

"I wanted to come see you," I smiled.

"Siobhan, it's nearly ten at night."

Before me father could scold me over the late hour, me mother's voice piped up from within the house. "Who is that? Who's at the door?"

Me father frowned but answered his wife. "It's Siobhan. I was about to send her off."

"You'll do no such thing!" me mum appeared in the doorway. She smiled when she saw me. "Come inside. Did you get off work and walk all the way here alone? The streets aren't safe this late at night, dear."

"Thanks, mum." I stepped past me father.

"Corri, it's nearly ten. The kids are in bed. We have work in the morning." Me father spun on me. "Siobhan, I know you work late, but you can't just show up at all hours."

"It's the only time I can get away. Work runs into the evening, and I have me nights off," I said.

I was more than a little agitated. I'd come all this way.

"Fergus, first you chastise her for not coming to see us, then you complain she's coming by too late. You know well and good, she works all day long. You should be happy to see her."

Defeated, me father put his hands up. "I am, I am. Of course, I am." He turned to me. "I thought you were sick. Your mother said you coughed up blood."

It had only been a few nights since me episode with eating food. I gave a quick nod. "I'm feeling much better. No longer contagious."

"Let me wake up the kids," me mum said.

"Corri, the kids have school, and Bradon has work. We can't—"

"They can go back to sleep after Siobhan leaves. They'll want to see their sister," me mum retorted.

Me father threw his hands up in the air. "I've lost control of me own house."

I moved to him and wrapped me arms around him. "Dad."

He let out a long breath and returned the embrace. "It *is* good to see you, Siobhan."

Me mum tore off into the room where me siblings slept. With only three of them together, it must have been a lot less cramped, I wagered. I could hear her whisper to me brother and sisters to wake up.

Murmured confusion and groggy questions were soon followed by excited whoops as me sisters charged from the room. Me brother trailed behind them, rubbing his eyes.

Moira was full of questions. Me living in high society had her enamored with it all. I reminded her that I was only a laundress, and I did not attend lavish parties.

I hated lying to her.

Fiona hugged me at the hips, and I gave her head a pat. She finally got to ask her own questions when Moira was satisfied.

"Can you really best Bradon in a fencing match with shillelaghs?"

"No," Bradon deadpanned.

"Don't know," I said. "Never tried." I winked at me little brother. He frowned at me.

"We were sound asleep, Siobhan," he complained.

"I want a shillelagh too!" Fiona shouted.

"Shoosh, Fiona," me mum scolded in a quiet voice. "You'll wake the O'Bradys."

"She'll wake the Murphys." Bradon scoffed.

The O'Bradys were on the second floor. The Murphys were on the third. Fiona responded to the implication by shoving her older brother, keen at stomach level.

"Oof! Fiona!"

"Shoosh, Bradon!"

"She just... it was her!"

"Thanks for this," me dad chided me.

I grinned and leaned forward to hug his shoulders. "Aw, you're welcome. Feels like I never left."

Dad patted me back. "Eh," he acquiesced. "You're always welcome here, me *cailín*."

"I thought I was your *cailín*," Moira affected a pout.

"You're both me girls!" Dad laughed.

"Are you getting a shillelagh, Siobhan?" asked Fiona.

"Well... no." I turned to me father. "What's got her all on about shillelaghs?"

A smile broke Bradon out of his sleepy frump. "Dad's takin' me out of the city Saturday. We're going to find a good oak root and dig it up."

Me mum shook her head. "Carrying those sticks around is just asking for trouble. It isn't like we're fighting in factions these days."

"No, but the Know Nothings linger around the docks, and they cause trouble. Better to keep the boy armed. The Yankees are cowards. They try to single us out and gang up on us."

Mum turned her attention to me. "Your father's been taking his own shillelagh to work these days."

"Actually, I can't blame him," I said.

Me mum gave a disapproving head shake.

"That's me girl," said dad.

"Dad's right. They gang up on us, and the police are no help. We're just as likely to get beaten up by the police," I added.

Dad swept his hand towards me to underscore me point.

Mum settled her eyes on the family. "May we please talk about things more pleasant for the short time Siobhan is here? It's bad enough we've got Fiona worked up into a tizzy."

The conversations turned to more pleasant things. Dad and Bradon talked about work, the girls talked about school, me mum threw in some neighbourhood gossip.

I was transported to a time before me curse. I'd barley registered it had gotten on past eleven. Time slipped away, and I felt right as rain.

I was home again, and I didn't want to leave.

I didn't want to say goodbye.

Me father stretched at last, making a show of it. "Well, I think we all should be getting some sleep, yes?"

Even me mum acquiesced. "Yes, I suppose so. Children, say goodbye to your sister."

I got hugs from Moira and Fiona. Bradon inclined his head to me, and I returned the gesture.

"I'll want to see that shillelagh when you carve it into shape," I said to Bradon.

It sort of slipped out. I was supposed to be telling them I was moving away and saying me last goodbyes.

"Come by Sunday," Bradon said. "I should have it well shaped by then."

"Oh, yes! Come by Sunday. For dinner." Me mum interjected.

I gave a wan smile. "Might not make dinner. Working and all, but perhaps after."

Perhaps I'd tell them on Sunday.

Perhaps.

Return To Crocus

"Do you have any idea what time it is!" William roared.

I stood in the greeting room as me creator's barrage of worry-fueled anger washed over me. I couldn't meet his eyes. There was no excuse I had that could placate his fury.

I'd visited me family in exchange for the tongue lashing I knew I'd get, but now that I was getting it, I wondered if going to see me family was worth it.

"I was worried sick about you! I thought you may have been discovered. I worried fae guardsman found you, that Esteban was making his move. What took you so long?" he bellowed.

I didn't want to mention the fact that I'd run into Lucy on the way to the North End. She was already being hunted and William had no cause to protect her. I also couldn't use her as an excuse for disappearing for hours on end.

"I…" I had to phrase this right. I debated lying to him. I debated concocting some wild story that had me unavailable to return at a reasonable hour.

William threw up his hands. "You went to see them, didn't you?"

I could only nod. I was still unable to meet his eyes.

"God Dammit, Siobhan! We talked about this!" he yelled. "Why can't I make you understand? We need to keep our noses clean, now more than ever. The wheels of the fae courts may move slow, but if Don Esteban has us dead to rights fraternizing with mortals and risking exposure, he'll have cause to move against us immediately."

"He'd move against me, not you. I've got me *aibíocht*," I said in a small voice.

His mouth fell open. "We are connected, you and I. Esteban is no fool. And do you honestly think that, even if we weren't so entwined that I'd want to see you punished for this? Is that your defense, that this might not affect me? That scenario is of no comfort, Siobhan."

I finally met his gaze. "They're me family."

"We've been through this. What am I going to do? What am I supposed to do to make you stop going there and risking so much?"

"I won't go again."

"You've said that before. You've lied to me."

He closed his eyes, and an uneasy silence fell between us. The tension that lingered was an almost tangible thing, like swimming in anxiety.

"Just go. Go up to your room and turn in for the evening. Tomorrow night, you need to go to your meeting with Madam Poppy. I want you to go there, meet with her, and report back to me. Do you understand?"

"Yes," I whispered.

He held me in his gaze a moment longer, scowling at me. "I am severely disappointed in you."

I had no defense. There was nothing I could say to make him see me side of things. He could never understand how much I'd risk for a family I loved so dearly. So, I brushed past him and hurried up the stairs to me apartment.

I resigned meself to spend the remainder of the evening to stew in a cocktail of guilt, anger, and misery.

The next night I was up and dressed about an hour after dusk. The heat from the receding sun still baked through the windows, but the danger had passed beneath the horizon.

William wasn't around. He was either asleep or didn't want to see me. I wondered if he had cooled off since last night.

Part of me was relieved. I was fine avoiding another fight. I grabbed the gold coin Madam Poppy had given me and struck out into the night.

The Crocus Tavern was an hour's walk. Among the several downsides of being a vampire was that we only traveled at night, while most of the city was shut down. All the horse-drawn buses were retired in the livery, leaving me to sojourn across town on foot.

When I got to Crocus, muffled piano music told me a night of debauchery was in full swing. I rapped on the door.

The little waist-high slat slid open, and two yellow eyes peered out. "Password?"

Dammit. I didn't know it. I stammered. "Um..."

The door slat began to close.

"Wait!"

The slat stopped, but stayed where it was. "Password?"

I showed me gold coin through the opening. "Madam Poppy gave me this."

"Hmph." The slat slammed shut.

Now what? Would I need to go back to William and ask him for the password?

The door swung open, and the goblin peered up at me. He was a different doorman from my last visit.

He shoved his hand up at me. "Coin, please."

I reluctantly handed it over. After a quick inspection, he looked up at me and said, "Come with me."

The Crocus Tavern wasn't originally a tavern. The two-story edifice was once a small apartment building. Many of the interior walls that divided the apartments were knocked down to create large rooms for gatherings and live feedings.

The upstairs rooms were reserved for private feedings. Rumour had it, the elite and wealthy among the bleed fed up there. With the privacy they had, unspeakable acts of bloodletting were performed.

I'd never been upstairs before. It never interested me, but that's where the goblin led me.

"I don't understand. Why are we going upstairs?" I asked.

"That's a silly question for someone bearing one of the mistress' gold coins." He stopped and looked me over. After a moment, he gave a grunt.

"What?"

"Just making sure, ye are what ye seem." He gazed up the stairs again. "Madam Poppy's got an office upstairs. I'm takin' ye to her."

I followed him the rest of the way in silence. We passed a couple of doors along the way. I heard moaning within one of them. From inside another, I heard whimpering and the distinct plea of *please, help me.*

"Is she alright?" I asked as we passed the door.

The goblin only grunted.

He finally stopped at a door at the end of the hall. The little doorman knocked in four even beats. Then two. Then three.

"Come in," came Poppy's voice.

The goblin swung the door open and stepped aside. "Enter and present yer coin."

I did so, feeling a little foolish. Poppy sat behind a desk, and she gave a quick glance at the coin in me hand.

"Leave us," Poppy said to the goblin. "Siobhan, sit."

I stepped into the room and noticed Poppy wasn't alone. Ian Hayworth sat across from her. I took the chair beside him.

The door closed behind me.

Madam Poppy's office was small. Her large wooden desk took up most of its width, and it seemed like the petite woman was drowning behind its girth.

The walls were a bright purple on top, bisected by a bright green chair rail running around the room's perimeter. Beneath the rail were green wooden panels. It was traditional architecture but painted in garish colors.

Fae.

"Hello," I said, breaking the silence.

Ian looked perplexed. "Where did you get that?"

Poppy leaned forward and held her hand out. I returned the coin to her. "I gave it tae her, of course."

Ian frowned a little.

"She slipped it to me at the party the other night," I provided.

Ian looked between Poppy and me. "I'm surprised she trusted you enough to give you that. We'd only just met you."

Poppy answered in me stead. "I dinnae ken about trust, but I confided in her. I told her I hated it here, working at Crocus and doing things for the *Scáilic Predominance*."

"You *told* her that?" Ian asked.

Poppy shrugged. The curls of her hair bounced off her shoulders.

"I suppose I gave her some measure of sympathy," I said. "I grew up in Ireland, and I've heard the stories of *sidhe* me whole life. *Sidhe* are not meant to be soldiers, enforcers, or the proprietors of blood bars. They're meant to sing and dance and frolic under the great faerie mounds of their home."

Ian looked between us both once more. Satisfied, he leaned back in his chair. "Alright. Let's talk."

"We'll make this quick," said Poppy.

There are so many rules for conversing with fae, that I thought it best to keep me mouth shut until specifically asked a question.

"We both ken that ye are with William and Ivan," Poppy began. "The question is, can the five of us work together?"

"I think we have a common interest," I said. "A common goal."

"Do you even know what that goal is?" Ian asked.

I thought I did, but his asking made me doubt meself.

In me uncertainty, Poppy supplied more information. "The *Scáilic Predominance* is an ancient order, born of the *Tuatha Dé Danann*. The old gods burdened their mistake upon the fae, that mistake being when they cursed the first man to roam the night as a vampire. The fae courts formed the Predominance to help their masters police their mistake and keep you lot from overrunning the whole damn world. You know this?"

I gave a small shrug. "I've heard the stories. I heard it was *The Morrígan* who cast the curse."

Poppy frowned. "It was. Don't let William and Ivan turn ye completely against the fae. Most of them feel as I do. It's the fae courts that force us into these roles."

That made sense, but I wasn't sure where Poppy's diatribe was going. None of this was groundbreaking information.

Ian answered me unspoken question. "To free us all, vampire and fae, Don Esteban must die."

Me mouth fell open a bit. Ah, there was the hitch.

"Ye understand, Miss McQueeney? Cut off the head of the snake and the rest can be routed out in short order," Poppy said.

It took me a moment to realize she was waiting for me to answer. "Yes." I blurted out. "Yes, I understand."

Both Ian and Poppy eyed me thoughtfully while I digested their information.

"So, you'll help us? Help us... kill him?" I asked.

"I won't risk Poppy."

"Ian!" scolded the fae.

I looked between them both. Ian furrowed his brow at Poppy. Poppy tightened her lips and stared back. Ian tilted his head at her. Poppy flashed him a wide-eyed look of insistence.

Their unspoken conversation revealed a lot about these two.

They were in love.

"Perhaps," I said, breaking the tension. "I could get word back to William and Ivan. We could all meet and discuss the matter."

They both tore their attention from each other and looked back at me.

"That is agreeable. Aye. Take this news back tae your creator. Ian and I have our own matters tae discuss."

Oof. Poor Ian.

I didn't waste time rising from me chair and offering a small bow to Poppy. I didn't know how this stuff worked. Was I supposed to bow?

I had no interest in lingering around Crocus longer than that. I had to get back to William. I had to tell him everything.

Episode Eighteen

Grief And Rage

William wasn't around when I got home. There was no answer at his chamber door, and there was no note left for me. It wasn't completely unusual. Sometimes William went out. But oftentimes, he would leave a note as a courtesy.

I puttered around the house for a while. I was a bit hungry, but William was very clear about coming straight back after Crocus. I didn't want him to come home and find me absent.

So, I waited.

And waited.

It was about an hour later that William got home. I was waiting in the greeting room when he arrived.

William looked surprised to find me there. "You're here. I would have expected you to be at Poppy's meeting."

"It was short. They really didn't talk to me long."

He closed the front door and looked this way and that. "Tell me what happened."

William looked distracted or perhaps bothered by something. He seemed off.

"Are you alright?" I asked.

He furrowed his brows and looked everywhere but at me. "I'm fine. Go on. Tell me what happened."

"Ian was there. He was surprised Poppy invited me."

"Why *did* she invite you? No offense, my dear, but *aibíocht* or no, you are a *páiste* in their eyes."

I didn't take offense at that. I'd wondered the same thing meself. "Poppy said it was for the compassion I showed her. When she confided in me about wanting to return to Otherworld and live a life fitting a *sidhe*."

William chuckled, but it was an uneasy thing. "Only you, Siobhan."

"What?"

"Only you could gain a trust of a fae noblewoman by sheer compassion."

"Lord, I hope that's not true," I remarked.

"What else happened?"

"What happened to your trousers?"

William had a tear in the left pantleg of his trousers. Now that I looked him over, he looked a little disheveled in general. "Are you alright?"

"Erm... hunting got a little spirited. I'm fine." He waved his hand at me. "Go on."

"They want to kill Don Esteban. They are open to an alliance, but Ian wants to keep Poppy out of it."

William stroked his chin and shook his head. "Damn fool. Thinking with his heart and not his brains."

"I think it's sweet. They're in love."

"He's a fool!" William snapped.

I took a step back. I was reminded of how I had left things with William, screaming at me over matters of the heart.

He ran a hand through his hair. "I'm sorry. I didn't mean... things are going to get dangerous from here on out. Ivan and I are planning to move against Esteban tomorrow night. I want to see if I can get Ian to join us."

Panic washed over me. *Tomorrow night*?

William put a hand on me shoulder. "I'm sorry for yelling at you earlier. I just care about you, and I don't want anything to happen to you. These ties you have to your family are so dangerous. But this plot with Esteban..."

"It's okay. I'm scared too."

He pulled me into an embrace and all the anxiety over our argument melted away.

"I would be decimated if anything happened to you, Siobhan."

I didn't reply. The solace within his arms was all I needed.

"Did you feed? You'll need to be at your best for tomorrow night," he said.

I frowned. "I didn't."

"Siobhan, you were at Crocus. You should have fed." He wasn't angry but exasperated.

"I could hunt," I offered.

"I'm not keen on you going out alone right now."

"We'll go together."

William shook his head. "I need to find Ian and discuss our plans. When was the last time you fed?"

I made a face.

"Not two nights ago? The night you and I went hunting?"

I braced myself for another scolding, but it didn't come. William ran his hand through his hair once more, looking anxious.

"Fine. You may need your blood to heal tomorrow if things go poorly. Go hunt, but be careful."

"I will," I promised.

I didn't have it in me. Not that hunting was always something that came easily to me. Sometimes, I was hungry enough that my curse whittled down me concern for others. But not tonight.

Tonight, I was more focused on the fact that we were moving against Don Esteban. This wasn't something I was ready for. This wasn't something I was strong enough to do.

I was terrified.

Trying to lure some tavern goer away from his pub or seek out some drunken vagrant was the furthest thing from me mind.

I could be killed. Tomorrow night, I could be killed. Me blood turned to ice just thinking of it.

I should have said goodbye to me parents last night. That way, if I died, they wouldn't wonder what became of me. They wouldn't suffer. They'd just think I moved away and never wrote them.

That wouldn't be quite as bad, no?

William would rage, but if I was going to face possible death tomorrow night then, perhaps, I should say me goodbyes to me family now.

I had to see them one last time.

I turned around and marched north up Tremont Street with an anvil in me stomach.

The closer I got to me family's house, the more peculiar things felt. Something was off, but I couldn't quite put me finger on it.

The energy past Prince Street seemed on edge. People peeked out of windows, but didn't venture out into the street. The streets themselves were uncharacteristically empty for this time of night.

When I turned on to Sheafe Street, I saw a gang of young men and boys looking about. They marched down the road armed with shillelaghs and knives. One man had a hammer.

I picked up me stride. Something had the neighbourhoods stirred up.

I turned down me parents' street to find several people milling around outside me family's home. I recognized a few of me old neighbours.

"What are you doing?" I addressed the group as I approached.

I noticed a woman was weeping. It was me old neighbour, Mrs. McLeary.

"Oh, lass," Tim O'Connor said. Tim was me father's friend from down the road. He looked heartbroken.

I pushed past them. "Let me in."

Mr. O'Connor stepped in front of me. "No lass, you'll not want to see this." He put a hand on me arm.

Me heart was racing. I pulled away from him and shoved him aside. I burst into me family's home.

Me eyes played cruel tricks on me. I was seeing things. I was dreaming. The horror before me couldn't be real.

Me family laid strewn across the floor, broken and battered. Me dad and Bradon were close by. Me father held his shillelagh in hand. Beside them was little Fiona, clutching the fire poker.

Across the room lay me mum and Moira, bloodied and bludgeoned like the rest.

Me body shook. Me vision grew bleary with tears. Me stomach turned sour. I wanted to scream, but I was too paralyzed to make a sound. I stood, powerless, gaping at the nightmare before me.

I didn't want to believe it. I expected them all to sit up, as if to make me the butt of some cruel prank.

Me eyes swept the room again, hoping against hope. That's when I noticed it.

Written on the wall in soot were the words *Irish go home.*

I heard Mr. O'Connor enter behind me. "I'm so sorry, lass. We got a call out to the police, but there's no telling when they'll show. We have some neighbourhood boys out looking around for any Yankees. Know Nothing pigs."

Know Nothings.

Me curse was sometimes like an angry beast trying to break down a door. Other times, it was like a snake, slithering around me heart like a disease. This time was different. This time, me curse came to me like an old friend.

And I welcomed it. It didn't break down any doors. It didn't sneak past me defenses. It simply wrapped its arms around me in a warm embrace, and I felt it sooth me with its promise to kill every last person responsible for what they did to me family.

I didn't rage. I didn't bellow, scream, or cry. I simply stooped down and picked up me father's shillelagh.

"Siobhan...," Mr. O'Connor began.

I pushed past him, through the crowd of horrified neighbours, and out into the street.

"Siobhan!'

I ignored them. I gripped me father's shillelagh tight in me hand. Tears streamed down me face, but I didn't have time to address me grief. I needed to find them. Me curse gave me strength. It kept me focused.

And I was grateful.

I wanted to curl up in a ball and cry. I wanted to scream and wail and disintegrate into a blubbering heap, but me curse kept me feet moving. Aimless, but determined.

I didn't know where I was going. I trudged through the streets lost in me own head. Me curse suffocated the screaming inside me mind. Me senses stretched out, seeking any manner of clue that I could hear, see, or smell.

A dog barked in the distance. The nearby hooves of a horse clacked on cobblestones. I could smell dirt, smoke from a fireplace, and that certain stench of humanity that permeated the city itself.

Yet, nothing drew me closer to me quarry. Frustration mingled with me grief and rage, brewing an emotional cocktail within me that grew more dangerous with each fruitless step.

Salt air hit me nose. I'd crossed the breadth of the North End's peninsula and found meself approaching the docks near Long Wharf and the western banks of the inner harbour.

I strode up to the docks and stared out over the water. They could be anywhere by now. Me curse tried to rally me once more. The sight of me broken family flooded me mind. It wanted to spur me onward.

But I couldn't. Me knees shook, and I wanted to drop down and wail. I wanted to scream and let everything I'd been carrying cry out into the night.

I sank down, surrendering to me failed hunt and the death of me family. I was on me knees when I gave meself permission to fall to pieces. I closed me eyes.

The harbour washed back and forth against the docks. The rhythmic sound was soothing, and I allowed meself a moment to seek tranquility in its song. It was the only sound I could hear.

I stretched me ears further, to bask in the serene calm of the waves. It would be the only comfort I'd find this night. All I could hear was the sound of...

No.

Me eyes shot open.

Muffled laughter carried across the night air.

I got to me feet and trained me ears towards it. Me curse revived itself, hungry to suss out the source of it.

I followed the sounds of mirth along the harbour's shore. I knew this area. I'd been here before. I'd hunted here. Anticipation welled me in chest. I was close. I could feel it.

Tears fell as I picked up me pace. That cocktail of emotions threatened to bubble over as a rush of sorrow and hate slammed against me defenses.

But that release would have to wait. Sweet providence had delivered me to an outlet for all of it.

The India House Tavern laid before me once more. I wiped me eyes with the heel of me hand as I processed it. This was the same place I came to hunt all those nights ago. Before Nigel was killed.

A wooden sign posted on the door read *No Irish*.

I tore it off and went inside.

Episode Nineteen

Wrath

I gripped the *No Irish* sign in one hand and me father's shillelagh in the other as I entered the India House Tavern. A few patrons raised their heads to take me in.

Me curse was wound tight around me very soul. It reinforced me rage, me hatred.

They were laughing. Drinking. Oblivious.

I wondered if the ones who killed me family popped back here for a drink and a laugh. Perhaps I'd never know who among them was responsible.

I tossed the wooden sign on the floor. It clattered and spun against someone's stool. The man looked down from his perch to inspect the object, then up at me.

"You lost, girl?" he slurred.

This caught the attention of a few more people, who paused their own conversations to look at me.

"Lost?" I replied. "No. I'm not lost." I turned and twisted the deadbolt on the door. Me hand was shaking.

"No Irish," the man on the stool said. "The rules don't change if you take the sign—"

I moved to him in the blink of an eye. Me shillelagh swung, and I clubbed his head before he could finish his sentence.

Skull shattered, the man slumped, cracked his head on the bar, and crumpled off his stool. Blood pooled from his head.

"Jesus Christ! Jesus Christ, get her!" the barman shouted.

"Degenerate Irish bitch!" another man bellowed as he came at me.

He tried to put his hands on me, but he was easy to evade. I was much faster. Inhuman. Fueled by hate and the blood of me curse. I swung me club again and caught the man square in the throat. He only choked a moment before I finished him with a second strike across his forehead.

There was a brief, delicious moment when these fools had no idea what was in store for them. A fleeting few seconds when they held no inclination that they were facing something horrible. Something cursed.

But when the second body hit the floor, that sinking realization swept over the crowd. I could see it in their eyes. The panic. The horror.

Me curse was giddy for it. and I was not inclined to fight it. Even as tears streamed down me face.

I leapt at them. One by one, they fell. Me father's shillelagh proved to be a formidable weapon in me hands.

It started with shouting, cries of outrage, ethnic slurs, and other bravado. Their hollering soon disintegrated into pleas for help and blubbering for mercy.

I didn't listen. I broke ribs with me bare hands, drove the ferrule of me father's shillelagh through their chests, and bashed several more with the clubbed end to send them all to hell.

The last man made a break for the door. I hurled a chair at him. It shattered over his back, and he collapsed to the floor. A moment later, I was on him. I brought the heel of me boot down upon his head.

I was numb to the carnage before me. Me curse saw to that. It would not allow me to feel any measure of regret.

The barman sobbed behind his counter. He'd hidden, and in the massacre, I'd forgotten him. I rounded the bar and held me weapon aloft.

"Please... please. Don't kill me."

The faintest flicker of conscience wavered within me, only to be snuffed out by the darkness that held me heart in its merciless grasp.

This man was the proprietor of a place so filled with hatred, that even money was not welcome if it came from Irish hands.

I lowered me shillelagh to consider him. I wiped me eyes with the back of me hand. Then I remembered I'd promised William I'd go hunting.

I leapt upon him, sparing no ceremony and offering no charm. He was lucid when I pinned him to the floor and sank me fangs into him. He struggled in vain. I drank, spurred by the will of me curse. Without remorse.

He screamed as I drank, so I covered his mouth. His free hand pummeled me in futility. He was weak, and I was the devil.

I pulled away from him at last. I'd slaked me thirst, but I'd taken more than any mortal man could afford to lose.

Me little flame of morality struggled to ignite within me as I gazed upon his ashen face. Me curse was quick to refute any attempt to regain me sense of self.

I scowled at the man. I crawled upon him once more and wrapped me hands around his neck. One quick snap and the man received the mercy he'd begged for.

It was done, but I couldn't leave the tavern in the state it was in. The slaughter would raise too many questions. Me curse's final compulsion was to take the kerosene lamp on the counter and cast it upon the floor.

I stayed long enough to see the hardwood catch fire. Then I made me way outside.

Me curse, satisfied, slunk back into its depths. It left me without the embrace of righteous vengeance. It left me empty. Alone.

I'd lost them all. Jesus, Mary, and Joseph, I'd lost them all.

I turned around to see the tavern in flames.

I fell to me knees and screamed.

I barely registered me walk home. I'd walked in a haze of turmoil from the burning tavern and found meself at me front door.

Me family was dead, and I had murdered at least a dozen people.

I didn't know how to feel. I was consumed by rage, sorrow, and hate. But for the people of the India House Tavern, I felt nothing. I wrestled with the idea that I should feel guilt over me lack of remorse, but still there was nothing.

I could tell something was wrong when I entered me house. I stood in the greeting room. William wasn't there to chastise me for returning so late.

There was a chair broken in the middle of the floor.

"William!" I shouted.

No answer. I called his name again, but I was met with only silence.

A sinking feeling came over me. William could simply be out with Ian, but it was late and why was there a broken chair?

The door opened behind me, and Richard stepped in.

"Richard?" I let out a breath. It was good to see a friendly face.

"Shevon, you're home." He smiled.

"It's a nightmare. Everything..." I turned and gestured to the broken chair. Where could I even begin? Yet, something was wrong. Something more than all this.

I looked back at Richard. "Why are you here?"

Richard shook his head in amusement. "Ah, poor Shevon. You were never meant for this, I think. I'm not sure why William included you. *Aibíocht* or no, you're still a *páiste*."

I scowled at him. "Where is William?"

"Don't worry. You'll be with him soon." He paused and looked around the room. "So disappointing. All this scheming and plotting. Murder. And in the end, what? William and Ivan captured like stray dogs."

"What are you talking about?" Tears welled in me eyes.

"I'm talking about the great game! The plots of immortals such as we, twisting and revealing ourselves from the shadows. The intrigue. The excitement!" He grinned like a lunatic.

"You're mad."

"You will find after so many years, that adventure comes not from hunting or our depraved bloodlust, but from great plots between immortal adversaries. Though, alas, I suppose you won't ever know, will you?"

"Are you going to kill me?" I stepped one foot backward and raised me father's shillelagh.

He laughed. "Nothing so barbaric. And no, I don't like getting my hands dirty. They'll be waiting for you outside."

I frowned again.

"Go on. Take a look," he urged.

I moved around him, giving him a wide berth. I pulled the curtain back and peered out the window. Four men milled around outside me door. They were armed with daggers.

No, not men. *Sidhe*. Me gaze pierced their glamour and revealed the horns on their heads.

I turned to face Richard. "Where. Is. William."

"The *sidhe* will take you to him. Staked and bound. To greet the sun on our great Bunker Hill and burn in a pyre with your fellow traitors on the legendary battlefield."

"You son of a bitch." I charged him.

Richard stepped aside and pushed me over. He was fast. He was strong.

"As I said, I'll not get my hands dirty. I'll leave that to the enforcers. Besides, I don't want to be present during any preternatural altercations. Let the fae expose themselves. I'll have no part of it."

I picked meself up. "Richard!"

"Goodbye, Shevon." He made his way out the door.

I wanted to charge him again. I wanted to grab his coattails and slam him through the wall, but I stood rooted on the floor with tears streaming down me face.

I'd lost everyone who mattered to me.

And now, I would be next.

I stared at the door as it closed behind Richard. Helpless. Powerless.

Beyond that door, four fae stood ready to apprehend me. I'd be outnumbered.

But I'd forgotten the umbrella stand. Me eyes wandered to it.

There it was. The Wheelock sword in all its iron glory, peeking out betwixt two brollies.

Episode Twenty

Outnumbered

I stepped outside holding the Wheelock sword behind me back.

Four *sidhe* were gathered around me front door, each with a dagger in hand. I didn't like me odds, and I lamented the number of layers I had on. The dress of a modern woman was not designed for swordplay.

One of them smirked at me.

The one to his left spoke first. "Siobhan McQueeney, ye are charged with treason against the *Scáilic Predominance.* Come with us, and we promise ye mercy."

Me stomach clenched. I scowled at the fae. "Burning to death in the sun is not merciful."

"I wasnae speaking of your punishment. I was speaking of your apprehension." He waggled his dagger at me.

I was at the end of me rope, and this absolute merkin was trying to be cute.

I withdrew the sword from behind me back. "Go to Hell."

"That's iron, that is!" another *sidhe* proclaimed.

The one who waggled his dagger at me narrowed his eyes. "Use your magic. She willnae be able tae get near us."

The four fae spread out and began to flank me. I stepped off me front step to give meself some room to move. "Magic didn't help Tailcoat Jack."

The one to me far right laughed. "The fallen one lost his magic when he became a bloodsucker. Ye will find us more formidable than he."

Me confidence shook at that. If Jack didn't have magic, then what was I up against? I looked this way and that. They closed in on me.

I needed to get out from between them all and take them out one at a time. Me eyes darted around, looking for the best opening.

"This is a waste of time," said the dagger waggler. "Tádhg, take her down. We'll grab her when she falls."

One of the fae, Tádhg I presumed, raised his hands above him. Wind picked up all around. Strong gusts erupted from his very palms. It blew me dress and threatened to undo me hair. The other fae backed off as the gale picked up strength.

I moved on him, trudging against the buffeting blasts.

The winds strengthened, and I was pushed back. I found it hard to move forward. For every step I took, I was pushed back two. The other *sidhe* were laughing. One of them was speaking, but I couldn't make out what he was saying over the roar of gusts assaulting me.

Me knees bent, and I put a hand on the street. It was difficult to stand.

"Ye may have defeated Jack!" one of the fae shouted over the storm. "but ye've not faced true *sidhe* magic!"

I stumbled. Two of the *sidhe* took steps towards me, but I forced meself to me feet again. They were ready to jump me the moment I was down, and I couldn't stay up much longer.

Me doorway wasn't far from where I'd stepped away. I grabbed the side of the building and pulled meself back onto the front step.

"Crush her against her own door!" another fae shouted.

The winds knocked me back and I slammed into me front door. I was pinned. I tried to step forward, and I found meself stuck like glue. The howling blasts of air continued to drown out anyone who wasn't shouting.

But I was exactly where I wanted to be.

I reached behind me back. I fumbled around until I found the latch to the door. I pushed it down, and the door swung open. The violent winds shoved me back into me house and sent me careening across the greeting room.

Despite the abuse I'd taken, I'd managed to keep hold of me sword. The winds roared into the house, but I was out of their path. I got back on me feet and dashed into an alcove where William displayed a small table and vase.

"Dammit, go in after her," came an exclamation from outside.

I peeked around the corner of the alcove and saw Tádhg pass over the threshold.

"Where are ye, lass?" He took a few steps towards the staircase. "Up the stairs, eh? Ye've trapped yourself!"

I leapt from the alcove and brought the sword down upon his shoulder. The dull blade did little to cut him, but the bludgeoning iron weapon ripped open his coat and brought metal to flesh.

Tádhg screamed and whirled on me. He moved his hands over his head once more, but I was too close. I swung the blade around and thrust it through his stomach.

He wailed again as the other three *sidhe* burst into the house.

"Tádhg!" Dagger Waggler shouted. "Kill her!"

"How?" one of them protested. "She's got iron and there are nae plants around for me to control!"

Tádhg slid off me blade and hit the floor. Soon, the firefly lights began to consume his body. I stepped over him and faced the others as Tádhg's body faded away.

Me heart was racing. For the first time, I felt hope.

Two mangy dogs trotted into the house and flanked the third *sidhe*. They raised their hackles and snarled at me.

The one who lamented about plants gave the dog tamer a pained expression. "Dogs?"

"We arenae exactly in the forest, are we? Nae like I could summon a bear or a wolf. Best I could do was these strays," he retorted.

"Shut up, you two. Faolán, set your dogs and bring her down," Dagger Waggler ordered.

With a snap of Faolán's fingers, the two dogs stalked towards me.

I didn't want to kill a couple of innocent stray dogs, under fae influence or not. I backed up towards the staircase.

Anxiety filled me chest, but I forced meself to keep me wits. I had to stay sharp.

Plant Lover was a few paces ahead of Dagger Waggler. Faolán was behind the other two. The dogs charged, and I made me move.

I leapt backwards, landing against the outside of the staircase. I briefly gripped the banister to keep from falling back down, and I planted me feet against the edge of the steps. Beneath me, the dogs jumped up and nipped at me toes.

I launched meself from the staircase, careful not to bang me head on the ceiling. I hurled meself over the dogs. In any other circumstance, it must have been a comedic thing to see, a woman sailing through the air, bustle ragged, bun unkempt, and sword in hand.

I slammed into Plant Lover, plunging me sword into his chest. His shrill scream nearly broke me eardrums as he and I crashed to the floor.

The dogs were on me, and I pulled the Wheelock sword from the hapless fae. His body began to glow in the throes of death.

One of the dogs bit me arm. Another latched onto the hem of me dress. Me arm stung like fire, and the second dog kept me from advancing on the other two *sidhe*.

"Morrígan's tits, ye are harder to take down than your creator," Dagger Waggler groused.

He turned to his remaining compatriot. "Once they've pinned her, slit her throat. That'll keep her while we package her up."

The words *slit her throat*, paused me concern over the stray dogs long enough for me to kick the one at me hem and launch the one on me arm at Dagger Waggler. With a swing of me arm, the poor pooch lifted off the ground, lost his hold on me arm, and crashed into the fae.

As much as I wanted to vanquish Dagger Waggler next, I knew I needed to get these dogs off me. I charged across the room at Faolán. He moved his dagger to block with one hand and snapped his fingers with the other.

"Get her! Get her, you filthy hounds!"

As decrepit as the Wheelock sword was, a dagger was no match for its reach and build. A few quick parries and I managed to swipe the tip of the blade across the fae's throat.

I stepped back to assess the temperament of the dogs. Without Faolán's prompting, they looked lost and timid. Both dogs fled from the house.

Faolán clutched his throat and fell to his knees. The glow of faerie lights consumed his body.

I pointed me blade at the last of them. Dagger Waggler.

He looked around the room, taking the time to witness the fading glow of the last of his companions. He scowled at me. His eyes burned with hatred.

He dropped his dagger and reached within his coat.

I wanted to charge him, but something about him had me uneasy. I hesitated when I shouldn't have.

Dagger Waggler produced a small tin whistle. He brought it to his lips.

I didn't know whether to be frightened or amused. Was he going to play me a tune?

And play he did. I'd never heard such beautiful music come from someone with so much hate in their eyes.

His talent aside, it was a foolish thing to do in the heat of battle. I brought me sword to bear, but I couldn't bring meself to attack him.

All I wanted to do was listen to his wonderful song. Me sword drooped in me hand.

The *sidhe* walked out of the house, playing as he went.

I followed.

It was a small comfort to hear such enchanting music. The horrors of the night melted away, and I allowed meself to take a measure of time to feel at ease. I needed this. It was a reprieve from all me suffering.

We made our way out into the street. His song continued, and I followed him to keep it present in me ears.

A woman stepped out in front of us. I recognized her.

The fae kept playing but looked quite dismayed. His song changed, and he pointed the instrument at the woman.

She looked unimpressed. How could she not be moved by such amazing music?

I recalled her. She was Lucy, the woman whom I'd untied from Nigel's chair all those nights ago. The woman who warned me I'd be attacked.

I *had* been attacked. The fae with the whistle and his friends attacked me.

But no, there was music, and I didn't want it to stop.

Lucy snatched the whistle from the fae's mouth.

"No!" the *sidhe* protested. "How? How did ye resist my song?"

Lucy frowned at him. "Your music can't charm me."

"Wait. I—"

I ran the Wheelock sword through his back and out his chest.

Me head was clear.

The death glow took the fae before he fell. In a gruesome display, he slid off me sword and crumpled to the street. Lucy and I watched in silence as the *sidhe's* body dissipated.

When the glow faded, I looked to Lucy. "How did you find me?"

"I told you, I'm a seiren. We sometimes get glimpses of the future. Earlier tonight, I had another vision and saw your attack. I came to find you."

"Thank you."

Lucy gave a quick nod. "Our fates are entwined." Then she inspected the tin whistle in her hands. "May I keep this?"

"Be me guest," I smirked.

She slid the instrument within the folds of her dress.

"Wait." Realization struck me in the aftermath of it all.

"What? Did you want the flute?"

"No. It's William. The *sidhe* said they took William and Ivan to Bunker Hill. They had them staked and tied up for sunrise."

The seiren furrowed her brow. "Bunker Hill's across the city."

"I have to rescue them."

"Siobhan, you're not hearing me. It's nearly four in the morning. Bunker Hill is miles away. You'll never make it before the sun comes up."

"William is the only family I have left. I can't leave him."

"You'll die."

It was a sobering thing to consider. I could never walk there and make it back home in time. Lucy was right about that. I needed a plan.

"You could go," I implored.

"Siobhan, I like you. I do. But there is no way I'm going to unstake two hungry elder vampires by myself. I'm sorry."

I bobbed me head at that. I remembered what Nigel did to her.

Then it came to me. "I can't leave them, but I can't beat the sun, either. It has to be me who unstakes them, but I still need your help."

Lucy considered me a moment. "Fates entwined, eh? Alright. Tell me your plan."

Episode Twenty-One

Out Of Time

"There isn't enough time," Lucy said.

"No. We can do it," I insisted. "We just need to split up. You get the carriage; I'll go to Bunker Hill."

Lucy put a hand on me arm. "Siobhan, there isn't enough time. The sun will be up in a little more than an hour."

"Let me worry about that. Please, get the carriage and meet me at Bunker Hill. And bring blankets."

"Blankets? Why would—oh! Yes, I understand. I'll bring the thickest I can find."

With no ceremony or farewell, I turned and ran.

"Good luck! I'll come find you!" Lucy shouted at me back.

I no longer cared about preserving the secrets of our kind. What would they do, execute me? I had nothing to lose, and I had to get to Bunker Hill before the sun came up. I ran at top speed, holding the hem of me skirt up as I dashed down the street.

Yet as fast as I was, I wasn't fast enough.

William had once told me that some vampires were so fast, they could outrun a horse. But not me. I was young and, although much faster than any mortal, I was a far cry away from the speed of a horse.

I sprinted as fast as I could to the livery to remedy that problem.

I raced down Albany Street and took a sharp turn on Essex Street. The livery was just outside of Common. It was not ideal to run so fast with me skirts and bustle, but the billowing fabric was more annoying than anything else.

The Wheelock sword was still in me hand. I didn't want to leave it behind in case I ran into more fae along the way, but the iron weapon was cumbersome in me hand as I sprinted across the city.

The livery was a barn-like structure outside the Common. It was the only building on the park's south side. I could smell the horses, but it was completely dark inside the structure.

This was where horses used for buses and other town transport were housed. It had been years since I'd ridden, and it was another reason to lament me layers of skirts.

The door to the stable was bound by a chain and lock. I hadn't really thought this through.

I regarded the sword in me hand. It was neither axe nor hammer, but perhaps in the hands of a vampire, it would do the trick.

I pulled back and whacked the lock with everything I had.

Not for lack of strength, but the weapon couldn't gain enough purchase on the lock to bust it open. It glanced off its side, and the doors remained secure.

It took a few more fruitless attempts at using me sword like a sledgehammer before me next bright idea.

I wove the sword through the chain itself. I braced the weapon on either end, careful not to cut meself on the edge. I twisted the iron against the chain, buckling up the links around its shaft and straining the entire contraption.

The sword bent under the pressure, and I feared the sword would give out before the chain did.

Then, one of the door handles broke free of the wooden doors themselves. The chain didn't break, but the strain on the handles was too much to bear.

Not what I was after, but I'd take it.

I withdrew the sword from the mess of chains and opened the stable doors.

The smell of manure, hay, and horses nearly caused me to step backwards. Me senses are heightened as it is, and this place was a punishment to me nostrils.

The horses, to their credit, stayed calm under all the noise I'd made. I wandered inside.

I didn't have much time, but I tested the temperament of a few of the horses before I chose a chestnut mare with a white stripe that ran down her nose. I couldn't find a bridle. I didn't want to spend too much time looking for one, but I found a saddle hung on the wall.

I was rubbish with saddling a horse. Me father always did it for me. But I grabbed the bulky leather object off the wall and slung it over the mare's back. I was grateful she remained so calm. I did me best to hitch it up properly, then I stepped up into the stirrup and...

Nearly fell off.

The confines of me skirt did not want me to swing me leg over.

I wasn't about to run the horse at full speed whilst riding sidesaddle, so I removed me outer skirt and tossed it on the saddle. Then I removed me bustle. I let that fall to the stable floor.

Unladen, I pulled up me remaining skirt and petticoats, stepped back into the stirrup, and swung me leg astride the horse.

Me outer skirt was still with me upon the saddle. I reckoned I might need that later.

I barreled out of the stable, doing me best to steer the horse down Tremont Street without the use of a harness.

The horse clacked on the cobblestones, and the buildings began to blur.

It was all a race against the sun. The night air grew hotter.

Me horse was amazing. I found I was able to press me hand against her neck, and she would turn in the direction I indicated. We sped down

Cambridge Street and then onto Commercial Street, and that wonderful horse kept me going faster than I could ever go on foot.

Though light had not bled into the sky, the heat became strong. I wiped me brow as sweat beaded from it, stinging me eyes and heralding the coming of deadly rays.

We tore across Warren bridge. I felt like I was flying. If not for the panic in me chest, it would have been exhilarating. I held on to the horse's neck to keep from sliding off. This wasn't my greatest idea, but she would get me to Bunker Hill before the sun came up.

I hoped.

Warren bridge emptied into Cambridge. Bunker Hill was still several blocks east. The early morning air was like a fire I'd stood too close to. The heat was uncomfortable, and I began to sweat profusely.

We sprinted through side streets and neighborhoods. There was no straight path to me destination. I'd run out of time. The night sky began to lighten, and the fire in the air became painful.

I ran east towards me goal, and directly into the oncoming dawn. The sun would break the horizon soon, and I'd be out of time.

If Lucy wasn't there with the carriage, that would be it.

I couldn't let thoughts of failure and death torment me. Me anxiety had me shaking enough as it was, and the morning's twilight started to redden me skin.

Bunker Hill came into view as I turned onto Monument Avenue. The hill was preserved within the neighborhoods that sprung up around it, and a short palisade of stone surrounded its perimeter in a neat little park.

I used the small stone wall to help me dismount. I wanted to hug the horse, but searing pain consumed me exposed skin. Me arms, face, and neck were burning. It was lighter. Daybreak loomed with every minute lost.

I pulled me outer skirt off the saddle and wrapped it over me head and shoulders like a shawl. I tucked me iron sword underneath it all and dashed up the hill looking for me creator.

I couldn't find them.

Shouting and cries of anguish carried across the open grass. There, coming from within the Bunker Hill monument, I heard the shouts of William and Ivan.

The giant stone obelisk stood over two hundred feet tall. I didn't have time to marvel at it. I raced into it, tearing open the door and diving inside.

"Siobhan!" William's cry was more surprise than greeting.

Beside him, Ivan winced in pain, but he couldn't hide the incredulousness in his eyes.

"You need to get out of here. The sun—"

"I wasn't going to leave you." I pulled the stake from his chest. William let out a loud *Oomph*. I set the Wheelock sword aside and got to work on his binds.

The shadowed confines within the obelisk gave some relief, but we had precious little time. I draped me skirt over William's head.

"Siobhan!"

"Shush. Hold still." I snapped the ropes that bound him.

"You'll die with us both," Ivan quipped. His face had been scorched red.

I moved to Ivan next. "Nice to see you too." I grabbed hold of his stake. I hesitated.

"What are you waiting for? Pull it out!"

"If I do this. If I save you, then my debt to you is clear. That business with Nigel, it's square. You and I are—"

"Yes! Yes! Forgiven! Anything you want! Just—"

I yanked the stake out with perhaps less care I had than me creator's, but I helped him from his ropes as well.

"Siobhan, why did you come? We're out of time. Staked or no, it's too late. The sun is here," said William from beneath me skirt.

As if fate itself aligned with William's words, beams of sunlight began to enter the monument from its windowed top. I shut the door to the ground floor.

The beams inched closer. Even without direct contact, me skin was scorching. I dropped to me knees and put me head in me lap. I folded me arms under me chest. It protected most of the exposed flesh, but even through the fabric of me clothes, the blistering heat was unbearable.

Ivan screamed. The smell of burning flesh hit me nostrils.

William was right. I was too late.

Episode Twenty-Two

The Cruel Sun

Ivan's wailing and screaming made it worse.

I gritted me teeth, trying to withstand the pain and keep me wits, but with each passing moment, the scorching light threatened to burn me alive. Searing pain ignited me body. The little protection me clothes offered no longer stood as a barrier for the sun's blistering.

William cried out over and over. "I'm sorry. I'm sorry."

I wanted to comfort him in our final moments, but I was too scared to uncurl meself and move.

At last, I cried out, wracked with pain and the guilt of me failure. I screamed and let the excruciation take me. I wanted so badly to be brave, but the scorching torment was more than I could bear.

Someone called me name in the distance. She sounded a million miles away.

"Siobhan!"

There it was again. I cried out, not in response, but from me own broiling flesh. The smell of smoke hit me. It was Ivan.

"Siobhan!" The calls were closer. Louder.

The door swung open, and twilight poured into the stairwell of the tower. We all screamed.

"There you are."

A weight landed on me back, head and shoulders. Curled up as I was, the burden draped over me and snuffed out the light. A thick, heavy blanket.

"L-Lucy?" I stammered.

"I got here as fast as I could," she replied. "I have a carriage waiting and... will you stop moving? It's a blanket. It'll keep the sun off you."

"Who are you?" snapped Ivan.

"Does it matter? I just saved your skin, bloodsucker."

"Siobhan, are you alright?" came Williams voice.

"I'm alright. We need to get out of here," I replied.

"I'll help guide each of you out," said Lucy. "Keep stooped down and keep the blankets covering as much of you as possible. Crawl if you have to. I have more blankets if we need them. I'll lead you into the carriage. It'll keep the sun out once you're inside."

"Who are you?" Ivan insisted.

"No questions," Lucy retorted. "Do as I say, and you'll get out of this alive."

I felt hands on me back. "Okay, Siobhan, get up, but stay crouched. Walk slow. If I take my hands off you, it means I'm leading some else. Hunker down and wait for me to guide you again. Understand?"

"Yes," gritted out. I rose up a bit, fighting against the pain. I shuffled me feet as I walked, retrieving the Wheelock sword along the way. Lucy led me out the door.

After a dozen paces or so, Lucy took her hands off me. "I'll be right back," she whispered.

I could hear her coaching the others. I lowered meself down and let the blanket cover me completely. Even within the confines of the thick wool, the sun was a terrible thing. The blanket offered some buffering, but it would do nothing once the sun began its ascent above the horizon.

The screaming stopped, but Ivan still moaned under his blanket. It was ironic that a vampire so much older and more powerful than I, was faring so much worse. I never wanted to be that far gone. I tallied this experience up as one more reason to not give into the temptations of the power me curse offered.

The process continued, and we each made our way towards the carriage. I was certain I was getting more attention from Lucy than the other two, but I was in too much pain to protest. I wanted to see William to safety too, but the blanket only dampened the pain, it didn't remove it altogether.

For what felt like an eternity, the cycle went on. Lucy guided me a few dozen steps, left me for a few minutes, then returned. Each of us advanced towards the carriage. I couldn't see a thing, and I was half tempted to sprint the rest of the way to get it over with. Sun be damned.

A brave thought, but the light gracing the grass around the edge of me blanket told me daybreak had arrived. Ivan's moans became louder and shriller.

"You're here. Step up," Lucy said. She guided me to grab the hand holds and place me foot on the step into the carriage. Hearing her say *you're here* was the sweetest words to me ears that I'd heard in ages.

It was dim inside the carriage, but with the door opened, I was still vulnerable. The pain began to ebb away, and I relaxed a bit.

Next, William entered. The carriage rocked as he got in.

"William?" I asked. I needed to be sure. I still had the blanket over me head.

"I'm here. Siobhan, are you alright?"

"Yes. For the most part. Hurts like hell."

"Shit!" Lucy called from outside the carriage.

Ivan screamed.

"Put your blanket back on!" Lucy shouted.

I was still unwilling to pull me own blanket off to see what was happening. "What's going on?"

"The other elder tried to make a run for it." Lucy's voice sounded further way.

Ivan hissed and cried out again.

"Get off me! I'm trying to help you!" Lucy yelled.

"That fool is going to die out there," William remarked.

"I'll go get him," I said.

"You'll do nothing of the sort!" William insisted.

The door shut and the carriage rocked. We were bathed in darkness. I pulled me blanket down. William was here, but there was no Ivan.

He was screaming outside.

"Lucy! Where is Ivan?" I called.

"Bastard tried to bite me while I was helping him along. I can't do anything more for him. And I'm not going to him if he's going to attack me."

"I'm going."

William pulled his blanket down. His face was badly sunburned. "No. You are not."

"I can't just let him burn to death!"

"You will die if you go out there! I don't care how well you can resist the sun, it's too bright out even for you. I won't let you go!"

"I came here to rescue you both, if I can't—"

Music.

Beautiful, unearthly singing filled the air.

I stopped yelling. William blinked and looked at me, bewildered.

The song had no words, only notes sung in an enchanting pattern. Unaccompanied by instruments, this wondrous voice arrested every thought and movement in me.

I didn't want to save Ivan. I wanted to stay, sit, and listen to the most enraptured singing I'd ever heard.

Ivan wailed.

Wait. Poor Ivan.

I leaned across William and dared a peek out of the curtains. Light stung me face, but I got a quick look at him.

Ivan was plodding his way towards the carriage. Smoke rose from his clothing. His skin was red and blistering. His eyes were squeezed shut.

He moved like a marionette, putting one foot in front of the other as if moved by an unseen hand.

The singing continued.

"It's Lucy. She's saving him."

Like sailors lured to the rocky shores, Ivan was pulled towards the carriage by the seiren's sweet song.

"William, put your blanket up."

He understood what I was about to do. "Be quick."

I pulled me own blanket over me and threw open the door.

The singing stopped, and Lucy shouted, "Get him in!'

I reached out blindly from under me blanket. Me hands grabbed onto Ivan. His arms felt like hot coals. I pulled him in, tossing him into the carriage once I had him.

I slammed the door shut.

Ivan howled in pain.

"We're taking off!" Lucy shouted from outside.

The carriage lurched forward, and off we went.

It took the better part of a half hour to settle Ivan down. He was in a lot of pain. When he wasn't moaning, he was nearly in tears.

The sun was a cruel celestial god that hated us for what we were. At least, that's how I saw it.

I felt horrible for Ivan's condition, but at least we'd saved him.

But now, he was staring at me.

"What is it?" I asked.

He took a moment before answering. His eyes searched mine for a moment, then he shook his head. "Don't ever let anyone call you a *páiste* again."

Ivan looked to William. "You chose well, my friend."

"Believe me, I know." William turned to me. "I must be the proudest any creator has ever been of his scion."

All this praise was going to make me blush. Not that anyone would notice. I looked like a beet. I simply waved me hand. "We're family."

William frowned and gave a quick nod. "Yes." He considered the word. "We *are* family. We three."

"Hear! Hear!" agreed Ivan. He winced when he moved.

The carriage slowed, and then lurched to a halt.

"Wait inside. It's not safe yet," came Lucy's voice. "I need to settle a few things, and then you three will be safe."

What did that mean?

William flashed me a quizzical look.

I shrugged. "I don't know."

The minutes passed. I was drowsy. The receding pain made it hard to nod off, but I'd been up all night and me body begged me for sleep.

The carriage shook again, and we lurched into a slow roll. I didn't want to risk peeking out the curtains. All my faith was in Lucy.

"Are you sure we can trust her?" Ivan asked.

"We'd all be ashes now if it wasn't for her," I said.

"Who is she?"

I didn't want to answer Ivan's question, but better Ivan heard the truth now, while he was powerless.

"She's the woman Nigel had tied to the chair, all those nights ago."

"The one who killed Nigel!" Ivan shouted. "Our lives are in the hands of that woman?"

"Nigel tortured her and starved her for days." I found me own voice rising. "Yes, she killed him. Would you have done any different to your captor? Lucy saved us. You most of all."

"That singing." Ivan frowned.

"Let it go, Ivan," William interceded. "She may have killed Nigel, but she saved your life. Her and Siobhan, both. The proverbial scales have been balanced."

"Nigel—"

"Nigel was a fool, and you know it. He reaped what he sowed." William leaned forward and continued. "This woman, this being, is better to have as an ally. She made you walk under the light of the sun to save you. Think of what she could do if she stood against us. Let it go."

Ivan gave a begrudging nod but didn't respond.

The cart stopped again. It swayed as Lucy climbed down.

"Okay, listen up. I have the carriage parked inside an old barn. There'll be extra protection from the sun in here, and it'll keep you hidden," she called from outside.

"We'll need to sleep for the day," William said.

"Go on. You'll be safe here. I'll be keeping watch, so go ahead and rest."

"Thank you," offered William.

"Thank Siobhan," she said flatly. "I did this for her, not you."

Lucy's footfalls crunched on hay and dirt and grew more distant as she walked away. The barn door creaked, and a heavy *thunk* indicated we had been closed in.

"At least she's honest," William grinned.

"We should sleep while we can. We need to end this later tonight," said Ivan.

William and I agreed in silence. I gripped the Wheelock sword tight in me hand.

When night falls, one way or another, this was going to end.

Episode Twenty-Three

Unto The Breach

I WAS THE FIRST one to wake the following evening. William and Ivan looked better, but their crimson skin was a badge of the horrors they endured. Their features were a bit sunken, and I imagined without their burns, they would look quite pale. Precious blood had gone into healing their damaged skin. They'd be hungry when they woke.

I dared a peak out the carriage's curtain. True to her word, Lucy had parked us inside a barn. The musty smell of hay and old wood filled the air. The only animal inside was a solitary horse, still outfitted in bearings and terret. Most of the old barn was barren, save for a rusty saw hung on the wall, a workbench, a plow, and a broken wagon wheel.

Moonlight streamed in from the gaps between the weathered planks of the wall. Whatever this barn was, it looked like it hadn't been used in years.

I unlatched the carriage door and slipped outside. I found Lucy asleep in the driver's seat. With the horse unhitched, the carriage's wooden shafts lay dormant on the ground.

I boosted meself up to the driver's seat, but didn't climb in. I needed to make sure she was okay.

Lucy's chest rose and fell with each breath. She looked peaceful, and she'd saved one of the blankets for herself to curl up under.

"Siobhan?" Lucy's voice was groggy.

"I'm here. I'm okay. We're all okay."

"Good. I should go. I don't want to be around when two hungry vampires wake up."

"Well, three."

Lucy sat up and stretched. "You wouldn't hurt me, Siobhan."

She was right. I climbed up and sat beside her.

"So, what will you do now?" she asked.

"I don't know."

"I can't help you more than I have. I'm sorry, but I had finally dozed off. I stayed up through the day to keep watch over you, but prior to that, I'd been up since three in the morning. I need to sleep. I can barely keep my eyes open."

"You've done more than I could ask. Thank you." I leaned against her.

"I never expected to have a friend like you, Siobhan."

"Nor I, you."

She pulled away and made her way down the carriage and to the ground. "We'll see each other again. Probably at a time when I'll need *you*."

"I'll be there."

I didn't know how all this fate stuff worked, but I aimed to repay me debt.

She gave me a wry smile. "Good night, Siobhan."

"What about your carriage?"

Lucy grinned at me. "It's not my carriage."

William and Ivan awoke nearly an hour after I did.

I could hear them talking and rehashing the events of last night. Apparently, they each fell prey to the magical powers of the *sidhe* enforcers.

If I hadn't had the Wheelock sword, they would have gotten me too.

The carriage jostled about as they climbed out.

"Ah, there you are," said William.

I smiled down at him from the driver's seat. "You're looking better."

I was expecting gushing praise from them both, but they each looked dour.

"What is it?"

"We need to finish this. Tonight. We need to take down Esteban," said Ivan.

"The three of us?" I asked.

"If that's all we have," said William.

I gave them both a dubious look.

Ivan stepped forward. "Siobhan, you killed Tailcoat Jack. You killed four of Esteban's enforcers. The three of us against Esteban should be sufficient, even for one as old as he."

I wasn't convinced. I heard rumours Esteban was turned in the 1600s. "Can we get Ian to help?"

"No time. And too risky. We can't afford to traipse around town. We need to hit Esteban's home directly," said William.

"The house that looked like a fortress?"

"It still has a front door," supplied Ivan.

"We need to feed. All three of us are low from our ordeal. Even you, Siobhan. I've never seen you look quite so pale," said William.

"How do we hunt? You said we can't wander around the city," I said.

"We're on the outskirts of town. Maybe we can find someone out here," offered Ivan.

We hitched the horse back up, and I was instructed to play driver while William and Ivan schemed inside the carriage. They were both still rough looking, with red faces and a few blisters. Ivan was the worst of the pair.

I drove us around country roads for the better part of an hour with no luck in finding anyone to charm.

"Still nothing!" I called into the carriage.

"Pull over," came William's reply.

He and Ivan got out.

"We're wasting night. We need to move on Esteban now," said William.

"Should we go to Crocus to find Ian?" I asked.

"It's too risky. The Predominance controls Crocus," me creator replied.

The three of us fell into silence for a moment. Then Ivan spoke. "Turn us around. Take us back into the city."

I looked to William, and he offered a nod in support of the plan.

"Once more unto the breach, dear friends, once more," Rallied William.

"I beg your pardon?" Ivan knitted his brows at William.

"He's quoting Shakespeare," I explained.

Ivan rolled his eyes. "Just get in the carriage, old man."

I parked Lucy's stolen carriage about a block away from Don Esteban's castle-house. I banged on the panel behind the driver's seat.

"We're here."

Ivan and William climbed out. They both looked wounded and bedraggled with torn and bloody shirts. Their skin had gone from red to sickly pale. Precious blood had done its job healing the burns and blisters, but their lack of vitae could be seen in their complexion.

I must have been a sight as well. Skirt and bustle discarded, dressed in an underskirt and petticoats. Me skin must have been pale too, for I'd taken me own fair share of burns as well.

I climbed down to join them both. The prospect of what lay ahead made me nauseous.

"What's the plan?" asked William.

"Esteban may still believe we're dead," said Ivan. "We storm through the door, find him, and kill him."

"Richard might be with him," I said. I climbed back into the carriage and retrieved the Wheelock sword.

"That sword won't cut anything," said William.

"It's iron. I told you, I believe Esteban is fae," I retorted.

"Fae?" Ivan nearly scoffed.

William shook his head. "Trust your senses, Siobhan. If he were fae, you would see it. There is no glamour and no fae features to see."

"I know what I saw. He burned himself on iron," I insisted.

"It's trivial. Bring the sword. It won't matter either way," said Ivan. "But Siobhan is right about Richard."

"We can handle Richard. Either you or I can—"

"No, we both need to stand against Esteban together. Either one of us and Siobhan won't be enough. Siobhan needs to face Richard," Ivan countered.

William frowned. "No. Richard is too old. Let me take him. I'll make quick work of him and then I'll join you both against Esteban."

"Didn't you two sort this out in the carriage already?" I asked.

They both turned to me and scowled.

"Richard is the wildcard," said Ivan.

"I'm not changing my stance. Either I face Richard, or this entire operation is over and Siobhan and I go into hiding. I'll not pit my scion against Richard."

Ivan shook his head. "You're too heart-strong, William. We have a bigger picture here." He looked between me and me creator. "Fine. Have it your way, you old mule. But I may not be strong enough to protect her from Esteban alone."

"He'll focus on you as he greater threat, and Siobhan isn't helpless. You two only need to keep him occupied while I dispatch Richard."

This was the best arrangement we were all going to agree on. The three of us made our way down the street to the home of Don Esteban Santiago.

We moved across Esteban's side patio and lingered by the door. Me heart was racing, and me stomach wasn't doing me any favours.

William looked at me. "Siobhan, no matter what happens, I—"

"No. None of that. You'll tell me when this is all done," I quipped.

"She's right. No time for sentimental nonsense. Everyone ready?" asked Ivan.

"That's not what I... yes. I'm ready," I said.

As I can be.

We burst through the door, smashing it into the house and breaking it free from its top hinge.

"Watch for goblins," Ivan said.

We entered the small side foyer where we had arrived for Esteban's party the other night. We made our way from the small room into the so-called function room. The opulent chandelier was unlit, and the room was dark.

Don Esteban's voice echoed into the room. "We found a cache of strange objects in the monument earlier this evening. Discarded stakes, broken rope, and strangely, a woman's skirt. No signs of fire. No ash. Nothing."

The three of us pulled together and gazed at the double doors that led from the large room into the rest of the house. It was the only direction Esteban could come from.

"I've underestimated you," the disembodied voice continued. "Especially the young McQueeney, I think."

"He knew," Ivan gritted.

"He was expecting us," William stated the obvious.

Esteban had time to plan.

The lord of the New England bleed entered first, replete with formal attire like he was hosting another soirée. Richard followed. Each were armed with a calvary sword.

William once told me fights between vampires were often done with swords. When beings such as we can regenerate our injuries, removing a limb can end a fight quickly. Removing a head can end things permanently.

I gripped me hold on the Wheelock sword. The rusty blade was a fine thing for fae, but against another vampire with steel, the dilapidated weapon was a sorry companion.

Henry Thatcher entered last, sword in hand.

Ian's scion was a known loyalist, whom Ian turned to make him a better man. The so-called former Know Nothing had allegedly amended his prejudiced ways.

I'd always known better of it.

"Henry," Ivan breathed. His eyes darted between our three adversaries.

We had just been bickering about Richard complicating things. Henry tipped the scales in a terrifying direction.

"New plan," William muttered. "Ivan, take Esteban. I'm on Richard. Siobhan…"

He looked at me, apologetically.

"I know. I've got Henry." I raised me sword.

Esteban laughed. "You've only one sword between the three of you, and you give it to the *páiste*."

That rubbed me wrong. Fear broiled into anger, and I snapped at him. "I was the one who rescued William and Ivan from the sun. I was the one who killed five of your enforcers, including Tailcoat Jack. I'm no *páiste*."

"Oh, ho!" Esteban chuckled. "Henry, my boy, do be careful."

Henry's lips slithered into a grin. "Oh, don't worry. I'll take good care of this little potato maiden."

Ivan advanced first, taking measured steps. "Once more unto the breach, dear friends."

William followed on Ivan's heels. "Once more."

Episode Twenty-Four

The Uprising

"It's time to crush your little uprising," Don Esteban said. His eyes narrowed on Ivan.

William peeled off from our group and stalked towards Richard. Richard raised his saber, but his eyes looked terrified.

Good.

I had me own problems to worry about. Henry Thatcher was making his way to me.

Me father taught me how to fence. It was with a shillelagh, but the movements were based on foils. Fencing with sabers was a similar art.

At least that's what me father told me.

I got in me stance. Knees bent. Hand at me hip. Sword en garde.

Henry laughed. "Oh, look at you. Standing in barely more than your petticoats and trying to look proper."

He lunged.

I parried. I kept me sword close to me body and blocked him with the low end of me sword, near the hilt.

He smirked at me. "Well done. Let's see how you handle this!"

He made a downward swipe at me temple. I blocked, but I didn't withdraw. I think he expected me to.

I could hear William and Ivan moving about. To me left, blades cut through thin air. I prayed they were alright. I wanted to steal a glance to see how they were faring, but I knew better than to take me eyes off Henry.

"I don't know where you learned how to fence, but I doubt you've ever faced an opponent as fast as I," Henry said.

He advanced again. This time, he was a blur of arm and steel. I did me best to parry what I could, but he was much faster. I concentrated on keeping me sword close to protect me throat, but I soon took cuts to me arms and across me side.

Me skin was aflame in the places he'd cut me. Hot burning pain sent daggers through me, and I had to fight through it.

I landed a hit on him, but me damn sword was so dull I may as well have been fighting with a shillelagh after all.

He forced me to withdraw, and he advanced on me.

I wasn't faster than him. I couldn't beat him. And he was slowly taking me apart.

I don't know what triggered me next thought. I reckon it's because I think of me father whenever I duel, which is something I'd been doing a lot of lately.

Me father's voice was in me head, chastising me.

Fencing is chess, he'd say. I was trying to match a faster and stronger opponent with speed and strength. Me dad would have cuffed me upside the head for it.

I had to stop thinking like a vampire and do what me dad taught me.

I parried again, but instead of striking a riposte, I weaved the Wheelock sword over his arm and twisted. I used the sword like a lever, the same as when I used it to pry the door handle off the livery.

That locked our blades.

With me free hand, I grabbed the hilt of his sword. I twisted the hilt in his hand towards his thumb, where the grip is the weakest.

One good wrench upon his hold, and his saber came free. I came back with it in me hand.

"How?" he stood, dumbfounded when he should have been withdrawing.

I slashed into his neck with his own sword.

He staggered and stumbled backwards. A mortal would have died. I'd nearly decapitated him.

It was a gruesome ordeal, but if I didn't finish it, his neck would be whole again. I advanced, spun, and brought the saber back through his neck.

This time, it cleaved through.

Henry's body hit the floor. I turned away, not wanting to look upon me own butchery.

I took stock of how William and Ivan were doing. Ivan lay on the floor, his head was twisted back in a sickly angle. William stood victorious over Richard, who had his own sword sprouting form his chest.

Esteban advanced on me creator.

William looked from our bleed lord to the sword within his reach, and back again.

I understood his hesitation. If he pulled the sword from Richard's chest, the git would heal all the quicker. Yet he needed the sword to defend against Esteban.

Esteban ignoring me and concentrating on William gave me an advantage. I leapt at him, a sword in each hand. I led with the steel sword.

Esteban spun and blocked me. It was an effortless thing, but I'd intended him to block. Locking swords with him, I swung the Wheelock sword around. He moved. He was fast, but I was careful to keep his steel confined against mine.

As he retreated, the tip of me iron sword grazed his neck.

He screamed.

"Iron," I said. "You see, William? I told you. He's fae."

Esteban scowled. He stepped back. "Congratulations," he said. "But your little discovery won't help you."

The vampire lord *slid* backwards. He didn't step. His feet didn't move. The soles of his shoes seemed to glide across the floor.

William pulled the sword from Richard's chest and turned it towards Esteban. "Impossible. What manner of vampire is burned upon iron and holds magic?"

It hit me. "He's half."

"Oh, very good, Miss McQueeney. Yes, I am only half fae. My dear mother. I look quite human, don't I?" he laughed.

Esteban moved to one side, but William crossed the room away from him. Why wasn't William moving to intercept him?

"Siobhan, where are you going? Flank him on the other side." William pointed his sword at thin air.

"He's over here," I pointed me blade at him.

Esteban's lips curled into a wicked smile. He turned opposite me and lunged. I heard the clang of steel as William parried, but the two were nowhere near each other.

I moved in and swung the Wheelock. It passed through emptiness, and the image of Esteban flickered before me.

William made a similar attack, his sword finding only space.

"Where is he? I can see him, but I can't hit him!" William called out.

Esteban's laughter was an unearthly thing, echoing around the chamber and coming from all directions at once.

William cried out. He withdrew a step. Blood dripped from a fresh cut on his arm.

We could see Esteban, but he may as well have been invisible. Wherever he stood was only an illusion.

Me creator frowned. "Ignore the mirage, Siobhan. Use your other senses."

An unseen sword skewered me shoulder. I cried out.

I withdrew quickly, expecting a follow up, but it never came.

He was toying with us. Taking us apart bit by bit.

Ivan stirred.

"Ah, the great conspirator rises once more," Esteban cooed.

Esteban swept to his right. His sword was met with nothing, yet the sound of steel on steel echoed in the large room. William was fencing for his life, yet Esteban looked to be fifteen feet away.

I moved against the vampire lord, but not where I saw him. I watched where William's parries were, and made a best guess where Esteban was.

I slashed out with steel.

Me blade hit something solid and came away with a slick coating of blood.

"Siobhan!" William shouted. "Get back!"

I ignored him and brought the Wheelock sword upright to guard me body. If William and I could gauge his placement based on his strikes, then we could—

I was stabbed through the stomach.

Across the room, the illusion of Esteban flickered and appeared somewhere else. He'd been right in front of me, and I never saw him.

I slid off his blade. Me stomach burned like the sun. I collapsed on the floor clutching at me wound.

"Now it ends," Esteban said from the corner of the room. Though, I was sure he was standing over me.

"You thought killing me would end your problems with the *Scáilic Predominance*?" he asked. "Europe will send more. Vampires. Fae. Perhaps ones like me, though I do believe I am the first of my kind."

A wicked slash appeared on William's shoulder. Esteban remained effectively invisible.

Ivan stood. He had healed the blistering damage from the sun and his broken neck, but he'd paid a steep price in blood. His skin was pale to the point of death.

"Your time is short. Even if we die here today, the *Scáilic Predominance* is fading. The fae are withdrawing from our world more and more every year," Ivan said, defiantly.

Esteban scoffed. "The fae lords take their cue from the *Tuatha Dé Danann*. And though they have withdrawn from this world, they are not without their means. You will never be free of their yoke."

I slid me steel sword across the floor to Ivan. To his credit, he acted like we'd planned it. He bent over and casually picked it up.

"Let us finish this. Then we'll see what the old gods have in store for us."

Don Esteban's specter looked this way and that from across the room. "I've toyed with you too long, it seems. No matter. You can't hit what you can't see."

His mirage made a lunge. We all reacted, for none of us knew whom he was truly stabbing towards.

Ivan twisted his body to one side, but the invisible blade raked him across the chest.

"He's there!" William moved and slashed into nothing.

"He's moved again," said Ivan.

I braced meself on the Wheelock sword to stand up. Me stomach still burned, and I was too low on blood to heal quickly. I feared I'd fall into the *death sleep* if I got too low.

"Back to back!" William shouted.

I did me best to hobble to them, hoping not to be stabbed again along the way.

That's when Richard got back up.

Esteban's laughter filled the room.

Me mind raced, and I took stock of our predicament.

Richard looked lost. He was robbed of his sword, and he stood doing nothing, bewildered.

The three of us had our backs to each other. If Esteban stabbed one, the other two could converge on him, but the old lord could easily withdraw faster than we could rally.

But I had iron.

That made all the difference. I swung me sword over and over, crossing me width, occasionally swiping down or up. No patterns, only random swings at the nothing in front of me.

If I was right, Esteban would not be keen on advancing on me while me iron skewered the air before me. He'd target William or Ivan first and save me for last, so he could stab me from behind.

At least, that's what I'd do if I were a tyrannical vampire fae in his shoes.

I kept me sword swinging.

"Once I disarm one of them," said Esteban from somewhere. "Pick up the fallen sword, then we'll dispatch the remaining two together."

He addressed Richard, but his befuddled scion simply stood wide-eyed and impotent.

What was he on about?

Ivan cried out, stabbed once more. William lunged his sword into the space in front of his friend but was met with only emptiness.

Me wild swings were staving off attacks against me, but it was only going to buy me some time. It wasn't going to save anyone.

William's words echoed back into me mind. *Ignore the mirage, Siobhan. Use your other senses.*

I closed me eyes.

I listened.

The fabric of me own clothes snapped and rustled as I kept me sword spiraling in all manner of thrusts, swipes, and directions.

In contrast, nary a sound came from Ivan or William, as they remained still and on guard.

Footsteps. Scuffing boots against the floor.

To me left.

Towards William.

I spun and brought the Wheelock sword up and over, slashing downward at William's flank and into the space before him.

Esteban screamed. His form shimmered, appearing in front of me creator.

"There!" Ivan shouted.

Esteban growled, withdrawing a step and slashing his own sword out. The blade raked across William's throat. Me dear William fell.

The lord turned on Ivan next, fast as a blur. He was visible, but he moved more rapidly than I could follow.

Ivan was overwhelmed. I came to his side, slashing out where I could, but the damn vampire fae was so fast, he could block each of our swipes in turn.

I'd underestimated him.

He never needed his magic to defeat us. He was faster than us all.

Ivan fell, clutching a gory slash across his chest.

Esteban spun on me. "You. Filthy. Little. *Páis*—"

A sword ran through Don Esteban's chest from behind.

Richard had run him through.

The lord of the New England bleed stood wide eyed and incredulous for one fatal moment. Long enough for me to run the Wheelock sword through his neck.

Don Esteban fell and crumpled at me feet. There were no firefly lights for him.

I met Richard's eyes. He no longer looked bewildered. His gaze was hard.

He dropped his sword to the floor.

"I didn't know he was fae," he said. "I didn't know he was one of them."

Epilogue

June 1864

Don Esteban Santiago was dead.

It had been nearly a year since William, Ivan, and I ended his reign, and his death gave us the freedom to expel The *Scáilic Predominance* from our territory.

I suppose I ought to credit Richard for his part in our liberty.

We never expected Richard to turn on his creator. He'd always been seen as a loyalist. Little did we know he resented the fae control over vampire territories as much as we did.

Richard was spared not only because of his involvement in Esteban's demise, but because he knew his creator's business. He knew the paths the fae used to traverse to and from Otherworld within our territory. He knew the shipping within the harbour where European vampires would travel the Atlantic boxed in coffins, to try to regain control of our territory.

Richard had mortal dockworkers seize those shipments in broad daylight, and many an ancient vampire had their coffins cracked open to greet the sun.

The immigrations stopped soon after that.

Ivan took control of the bleed in the months following Esteban's destruction. It was contested by William, which was a shame because the contest of power drove a wedge into their friendship that still hadn't truly recovered.

William, for his part, forged alliances in New York and brought their bleed closer to ours. Rumour had it, they'd been seizing control of their own ports and working to free themselves from the Predominance as well.

I'd moved out of our shared apartment, having finally gotten me due under me *aibíocht*. A small dowry from William kept me comfortable. I had a place just outside the North End near Faneuil Hall. Ivan worried about me living in the North End itself and forming mortal attachments. Apparently, he knew I'd kept ties with me family after me turning, and he fretted over me making the same *mistakes*.

His insufferable disposition aside, I had no interest in returning to me old neighbourhood. I couldn't. Me family had been laid to rest, and with all such ceremony that goes with it, I could not attend. The sun barred me from me own family's wake and funeral. I wasn't even sure where they had been buried. I was ashamed for having missed it. The grief still clung to me.

The only family I had left was William. Even me friends were running thin.

Such as I discovered when Lucy called on me to announce her leaving Massachusetts.

She came to me home some nights ago. When I opened the door, Lucy stood in front of a loaded coach parked on the street. Luggage piled upon its roof and a man sat in the driver's seat.

"Lucy," I was surprised to see her.

The moonlight graced her features under the evening sky. I'd forgotten how beautiful she was when she wasn't half-starved or when I was peering at her from under a blanket.

"How have you been?" she asked.

"Good, but it's been difficult. The Predominance is still sending fae into the territory. We're always hunting."

"I came to say goodbye."

"You're leaving?"

"For now. I can't stay in any one place for too long. I have the same problem you do. I don't age," the seiren said.

"But we vampires remain in our cities. Can't you?"

"You lot move around a bit and put a lot of effort into reinventing yourselves. Plus, you can't travel as easily as I can. The daylight and all."

"Where will you go?"

"Nevada. Carson City. I've heard the territory has built up pretty well. It's also far enough away that it'll be unlikely that I'll run into any of my mortal acquaintances from Massachusetts."

"Nevada," the name felt strange on me tongue. I'd always thought of anything west of New York as one vast, untamed wilderness.

"I'll come back around to Boston in a few decades. And I'll write you. We are friends, yes?"

I didn't have to think about that. "Yes."

"Take care, Siobhan."

Before I could return her sentiment, she pulled me into a hug. It wasn't one of those *ladies of society* embraces where they scarcely touched each other and kissed the air beside each other's cheeks. Lucy pulled me into a true, arms wrapped around me, hug.

I returned it.

Such displays were considered crass in polite society, but I didn't care. I came from a place where we showed what we felt and said what we thought. Lucy was a kindred spirit, and I welcomed it.

At last, Lucy pulled back and gave me a smile. "We'll see each other again, Siobhan McQueeney. Fates entwined."

I smiled back. "Fates entwined."

Also By J.M. Celi

For over century and a half, Lisa has kept the toll of her curse at bay. In doing so, she's maintained the remnants of the woman she was in life, but she has denied herself a great deal of power. Such a sacrifice can be dangerous in nights filled with supernatural perils. Matters complicate when a mortal becomes entwined in her life. How will Lisa keep her secret hidden from a new friend while protecting him from the horrors that threaten herself and everyone close to her?

Buy Online:

https://bookshop.org/shop/jmceli

Magic is never easy.

The Peabody Coven does things a little differently. The seven women combine dissimilar magics across their various cultures and methods. This CONVERGENCE allows the coven to create powerful effects wielded to protect and defend the Massachusetts territory.

When the coven's druid discovers a great evil in a nearby park, the coven must come together to combine their magics to vanquish a harmful blight on mother earth.

But what can corrupt the land can also corrupt the mind.

The Wicked Wound of Whitney Hill is a stand-alone short story that ties into the events within "The Unlife of Lisa Cooper".

Buy Online:

https://a.co/d/bcneS7v

About The Author

J.M. CELI lives in New England with his wife, son, and a small grumble of pugs.

Web Page: https://www.jmceli.com

Amazon Author Page: https://tinyurl.com/ynyvhnfh

Goodreads:

https://www.goodreads.com/author/show/23410446.J_M_Celi